WHISKEY TANGO FOXTROT

By
New York Times bestselling author

LILIANA HART

All tragedies are finished by a death,
All comedies are ended by a marriage;
The future states of both are left to faith…

~Lord Byron

Between two evils,
I always pick the one I never tried before.

~Mae West

For Scott,
Because you're my hero and my heart.

PROLOGUE

Tuesday…

I WAS USUALLY a glass half-full kind of girl. But I was pretty darn sure this was the worst day of my life.

Once, when I was eight, I'd decided to be Gene Kelly in *Singin' in the Rain*. I'd twirled and stomped through puddles with abandon, singing at the top of my lungs. I swung with gusto around a lamppost, tapping like mad as the rain poured from the sky. Until my galoshes got tangled—which is a polite way of saying I tripped over my own feet. I ended up flat on my back and my head hit a rock, knocking me unconscious.

My name is Addison Holmes, and I've hit my fair share of rocks. I'm a private investigator for the McClean Detective Agency, and I'm still new to the business. Meaning I get the job done, but there are a lot of other people at the agency that do the job better than me. For instance, if you were kidnapped and your life was in danger, I'd more than likely find you. But you'd probably be dead.

My stint as Gene Kelly didn't last long. When I came to, I had the mother of all headaches and my vision was blurry for three days. My skin was cold to the touch and I was shivering uncontrollably. But at least I had all my clothes on, which was more than I could say this time around.

I woke much the same way I had that fateful day when I was eight. The pain in my skull was like nothing I'd ever experienced and my vision was so blurry it took me several minutes to realize I was staring at a beige ceiling and not the gates of heaven, which was good news because I had much higher expectations for heaven.

I rolled my eyes from side to side because it was too painful to move my head, and recognition started to kick in—shower curtain—toilet—sink—dingy towels—tray full of sharp surgical instruments. One of those things didn't belong.

My gaze froze on the tray, and I felt panic start to take over. My teeth chattered uncontrollably and I couldn't seem to function—couldn't get my wits about me. Not having my wits about me wasn't unusual, but this time it was serious. I was in deep trouble. And my charm and adorable personality weren't going to get me out of this mess.

I stared into the tub and my lungs constricted. Blood pumped with a roaring whoosh in my ears, and I tried desperately to suck in a breath. I was naked. And buried in an ice bath.

High-pitched wheezes escaped from my lips until I sounded like a balloon having the air slowly leaked from it. This was not good. In fact, this was about as far from good as I'd ever been. If my tear ducts hadn't been frozen I probably would've cried.

I rolled my head to the side and tried to listen—to see if I was alone or if my surgeons were still present. But nothing greeted me but silence and my erratic heartbeat.

The sign on the door was crudely written with black marker, and it said, *Call 9-1-1. Now.* An envelope with my name written on it was taped just beneath the sign.

Bile rose in my throat and little black dots were dancing like dust mites in front of my eyes. It was everything I could do to keep the contents in my stomach down. If I even had a stomach. I had no idea what kind of wounds the ice was covering, but I was almost a hundred percent sure that vomiting wouldn't be good for them.

I looked at the surgical tray where there was supposed to be a phone, but there was nothing there—only sharp-edged instruments that mocked me. Panic clawed at me again. My ice was going to melt and I was going to bleed out, and I'd die alone in a bathtub in a three-and-a-half star hotel. I'd always imagined I'd die with a bit more glamour. It was kind of a letdown.

I couldn't die like this. My unwritten biography demanded that I not end my story this way. My only choice was to try to move. To escape the tub and crawl my way out to the hallway where someone might find me before it was too late.

I was going to fall apart at some point, but not yet. I needed to survive. I had things in my life I still wanted to do. Like make out with Chris Hemsworth and get laser hair removal.

I focused on my body and tried to move my limbs, even just a little. I managed to get my knee bent so it stuck up out of the ice bath, and it was then I noticed the plastic bag that surfaced with the movement. It took me a couple of tries to get my fingers to curl and pick up the bag, but once I did I was almost bursting into tears.

Inside the plastic bag was a cellphone, and there was only one person I could think of calling. Someone who would drop everything and come for me because I asked. Someone I didn't mind seeing me naked. Believe it or not, it was a short list, despite my twenty-four hour stint at a nudist colony not too long ago.

My fingers fumbled at the opening of the plastic bag and I prayed like crazy that I didn't drop it in the water. Getting out of the tub at this point wasn't an option. I needed whatever insides I had left to stay put.

Wild animal sounds escaped my mouth as I dialed with shaking hands. It seemed to take forever as the phone rang—and rang—and rang. Then the sweetest voice I'd ever heard answered the phone.

But when I opened my mouth no words came out. Just hot air and desperation. I was well and truly fucked.

CHAPTER ONE

Saturday

THERE ARE SOME days it's not worth getting out of bed. Today was one of those days.

Sirens blared in the distance, but between tourist traffic and people generally being assholes and not moving to the side of the road for emergency responders, I figured the cops still had a good five minutes before they got here.

A hysterical woman was Skyping with someone from Channel 8 News, reporting that shots had been fired at the Enmark Gas Station off Montgomery Street. Rosemarie and I had pulled up just in time to see the woman put on fresh lipstick and practice a couple of sobs before dialing into the station.

Over the last several years, Savannah's crime had spiked. Shootings and domestic disturbance calls were always going out over the radio. And this was the third gas station robbery this week. The cops were doing everything they could to keep things under control, but like with most things, when politicians got involved everything went down the shitter. So while the cops worked with their hands halfway tied behind their backs and buried in mountains of red tape, dodging bullets and putting their lives in danger, the rest of us got to watch the city burn. So to speak.

Shots rang out from inside the gas station and everyone hit the deck, myself included.

"Shoot that motherfucker!" Rosemarie screamed, a hysterical tinge to her voice.

We huddled behind the open doors of her bright yellow Beetle. On her best day, Rosemarie didn't do well in stressful situations. She'd shown up at the detective agency about half an hour ago, her mascara smudged from the night before and her bright red dress turned inside out. Her hair looked like she'd brushed it with a hand mixer, and I was almost a hundred percent sure she wasn't wearing a bra. Using the deductive reasoning skills I'd acquired over the two months I'd been a private investigator, I was willing to go out on a limb and say today was nowhere near one of her "best days."

"Ssh," I hissed. "You don't want to startle him into killing anyone."

"He's killing everyone. Didn't you just hear him unloading on all those poor people? They're just trying to get their gas station Danishes and fill up their tanks for a nice weekend away. And now they're all going to die." Rosemarie inhaled a deep breath and let out a *hee-hee-hoo* like she was in Lamaze class. Rosemarie was a little excitable.

"He's not killing everyone. He just fired a bunch of rounds into the ceiling. Kid can't be more than twenty. Looks scared to death."

"America's youth today," she said, shaking her head. "Be glad you're not teaching anymore. Everything's going to hell in a handbasket. I had a kid tell me the other day that Disney invented Pocahontas because they needed a Native American princess, and that she wasn't a real person like Wikipedia claimed. Took everything I had not to slap him right upside the head. In two years he's probably going to be holding up a gas station too. And what is that boy wearing? He's robbing a gas station convenience store in his pajama pants? And plaid pajamas at that. I hate to break it to him, but he looks like the *Brawny* lumberjack instead of a badass."

"Maybe he thought the wife beater and bandana tied around his head made him look tough enough."

"You'd think they'd have some kind of online classes for thugs," she said. "They've got online classes for just about everything these days. Some enterprising young man could monetize the site and probably make a fortune off all the gangbangers and lowlifes, teaching them how to commit crime more efficiently."

"I'm sure the Better Business Bureau would love that," I said dryly.

"Are you going to shoot him or not? I'm starting to get a cramp and I need a fucking donut."

"You sure are swearing a lot today. That's not like you."

"I've been watching marathons of *Mad Men.* It's a bad influence on my social niceties."

"I can't shoot anyone," I said. "I left my gun in the shower caddy at the office."

For the last week, I'd been calling the McClean Detective Agency my home. I'd been living with Nick Dempsey for several months before he decided to ask me to marry him and threw a wrench in the works. I'll admit I panicked. A girl who's been left at the altar doesn't think about marriage and weddings without fear rearing its ugly head. I thought I'd been very mature when I told him I needed time to think on it, and that maybe it was best if we gave each other a little space while I did.

In reality, I'd been avoiding Nick like the plague. Our lines of work often put us in each other's paths, but I had Nick radar. I could practically feel his presence before he ever arrived at a scene. I could also feel his presence because I'd stuck one of the trackers we used at the agency underneath his truck. My phone vibrated every time he was in a ten-mile radius.

It was really hard to give myself the space I needed to make an informed, adult decision. I knew what that man could do in bed, and my hormones weren't as informed and adult as my brain was.

"We're all going to die," Rosemarie said. "Help me, Jesus. Help me!" She threw in a sign of the cross for good measure. Rosemarie was Methodist just like I was, but I figured God might give her extra points for effort.

"Oh, for Pete's sake," I mumbled under my breath. Then I reached into the car and grabbed the box of donuts we'd just procured when the call for the robbery had come through on the police scanner. I slid the box toward Rosemarie and she huddled behind the door, her blue eyes wide and round like a Kewpie doll, as she devoured a chocolate glazed.

I still wasn't sure why Rosemarie had a police scanner in her car. Or where she'd gotten it, for that matter. Rosemarie taught choir at James Madison High School in Whiskey Bayou, but ever since I'd gotten my P.I. license she liked to think of us as the Southern version of Cagney and Lacey, even though she had no special training and had a tendency to overreact in high stress situations. In reality, we were more like a deranged Abbott and Costello.

"I'm just saying," Rosemarie said, reaching for another donut, "what good is a gun if you're going to leave it in the shower? I've got mine right under the front seat of the car. You can use it if you want to."

"I'll pass," I said. "The police will be here

soon." Not to mention the fact that I was pretty sure Rosemarie didn't have a concealed carry permit. But that didn't stop ninety percent of the Georgia population from carrying them anyway. Southerners weren't fond of things like permits.

"Why do you take your gun in the shower anyway?" she asked.

"I take my gun everywhere," I said, peeping around the car door to look inside the gas station so I could assess the situation. The more information I could give the cops when they arrived the better. "But I wasn't expecting you to use the spare key and disarm the agency alarms while I was trying to put my clothes on. And I sure wasn't expecting you to burst into the bathroom and drag me half-naked down the hall because you were having a crisis. So it got left in the shower caddy."

"I needed a donut," she said, pouting a little. "I had a rough night. I thought Robbie might be the one. After Leroy broke my heart I did what I read in Cosmo and had a couple of rebound flings. Then I met Robbie and my world tilted on its axis and all thoughts of Leroy went right out the window. I thought that was a sign that I'd found *the one*. And it was my first attempt at being a cougar."

"Who's Robbie?" I asked.

"He's that bartender we met last week at the nudist colony."

"Don't remind me," I groaned.

A week ago, I'd caught my first and last case that involved going undercover at a nudist colony. The experience had taught me a lot about myself. Mostly that I wasn't meant to be naked at the beach. There were parts of the body that shouldn't be exposed to sand and sun. I'd also discovered that I didn't particularly want to see other people naked either. There was nothing quite like watching the woman across the dinner table as her nipple fell into her soup bowl every time she leaned forward.

"You thought Robbie was the one?" I asked, perplexed. "You hadn't talked to him five minutes before y'all were going at it behind the tiki bar. How are you supposed to know someone's *the one* after five minutes? And three and a half of that was foreplay."

Rosemarie sniffed. "Sometimes souls just connect. It was like that for me and Robbie. But being at a nudist colony really takes away the subtleties of flirtation. I could see everything he was thinking below his waist. It's hard not to fall for such blatant seduction techniques."

"I take it Robbie doesn't share your soulmate sensibilities?"

"Robbie graduated from high school last year and still lives with his parents. They all live full-time at the nudist colony. He's not sure about working and living out in the real world. He said he likes the freedom of the nudist lifestyle and he'll miss his mother's chocolate chip cookies if he moves away from her."

"Jesus," I said, eyes wide. "He's practically an infant. Men don't know anything about pleasing women at that age."

Rosemarie frowned and said, "I've slept with a lot of men. I'm not sure I've ever found one that knew how to please me. I think it's a myth. Like unicorns. Or that picture that went viral on Facebook about the man with two penises. Anyone could see that second one was Photoshopped."

"Men that know how to please women exist," I said glumly.

I knew this because I'd just told one I had to think about an eternity of receiving pleasure. I was an idiot. I looked at Rosemarie and felt indignation rise up within me that none of her partners had been interested in anything but their own pleasure.

"You're a woman in the prime of your life," I told her. "What you need is a *real* man. An older man. Someone who knows how to treat you outside the bedroom and rock your world inside it. Maybe a widower or a divorcee."

"Where do you think I can find one of those?" she asked, intrigued. "Assisted living? Or maybe that retirement village down on Tybee Island? They're real go getters down there."

I didn't really have a solution. Indignation was about as far as I could take this particular problem. "Have you tried one of the online dating sites?"

"Oh, sure. I've got profiles on all of them. Everyone lies about who they are and what they look like, and when you finally meet in person you know you're only meeting for a quick hookup, so no one much cares about the lies anyway."

"That's horrible," I said, my faith in humanity slightly dented. "They always show those people getting married and so happy on the commercials."

"I think mostly they're happy they're getting

regular sex and didn't marry a serial killer. Those computer programs are pretty good at screening out most of the crazies. At least the ones that might kill you."

"Huh," I said and turned my attention back to the gas station. No more shots had been fired and the sirens were getting closer. I took a deep breath and peeked around the side of the door so I could look into the gas station one more time.

I wasn't sure what I'd been mentally preparing myself to see. I was past thirty, so it was under-standable that my eyes might not have been as good as they once were. In fact, I was praying that was the case. There had to be a thousand or so ninety-something women who wore fur coats over their velour jogging suits. There was no reason to think that my Aunt Scarlet was inside the gas station with an armed robber. She was supposed to be halfway to Italy on a singles cruise.

I peeped again and sighed. My eyesight was spectacular. And there was no mistaking Aunt Scarlet.

"Hey," Rosemarie said, coming back to ration-al behavior as the sugar hit her bloodstream. "That looks just like Scarlet. I thought she was headed out on a single's cruise."

"That was the plan," I said. "Maybe it's not her."

It was her. There was no mistaking Aunt Scarlet. In her prime, people said that Scarlet looked just like Ava Gardner. I'd seen pictures, so I knew the rumors to be true. I'm not sure what had happened as the years passed, but Ava Gardner started looking more like Mickey Rooney. She'd shrunk, so she was barely five-feet tall, and she had a shock of white hair she kept permed and teased so it added a couple inches to her height. She kept it shellacked so nothing less than hurricane-force winds could move it out of place. She was wearing a mink, floor-length coat that swallowed her and she looked mad as hell.

Scarlet Holmes was my father's aunt. She'd grown up in Whiskey Bayou and outlived five husbands, a couple we weren't so sure had died of natural causes. Most families had a skeleton or two in the closet. Scarlet was one of ours. She liked her men young, her whiskey neat, and her cigarette's unfiltered.

"Thank you. I feel better now," Rosemarie said, pushing the half empty box of donuts back toward me. "It's the stress. It makes me irrational. I've got a new game plan now. I won't even look at a man unless he's on the sunny side of sixty. Maybe Scarlet knows someone."

"Maybe you should get some anti-anxiety meds," I told her.

"I've got some, but I don't like being that relaxed. Two days before Christmas I was stressed because the home spa I'd ordered for my mother showed delayed shipping. And you know how my mother is. I'd never have heard the end of it to show up to Christmas dinner without *everyone's* gifts. So I schlepped myself to the mall two freaking days before Christmas. Holiday shopping always makes me a little crazy anyway, so I popped a couple of those pills and ended up taking a nap on one of the display couches in JCPenney. Turns out they thought I was dead and called 9-1-1."

I was only half-listening to Rosemarie. Pretty much nothing she said shocked me anymore. I was more interested in how to get my Aunt Scarlet out of the gas station alive. She was standing face to face with the gunman, but neither of them were speaking. The situation looked tense.

If I hadn't been so focused on Scarlet and the

gunman I would've felt my phone vibrate, signaling Nick's arrival. The second his hand touched my shoulder chills danced along my spine and my nipples went to full alert.

"Any donuts left?" he asked.

I'd forgotten how to blink, and I was starting to get a cramp in my calf from squatting too long. His voice rasped across my skin and my hand clutched the seat. I mentally ran down what I looked like. And winced.

I hadn't been kidding when I'd said Rosemarie had dragged me down the hall half-naked. I'd had time to put on a pair of black sweatpants, a thermal undershirt and an oversized Georgia Tech sweatshirt I'd had since college. I hadn't actually gone to Georgia Tech, but I'd dated a guy who had. It turns out I liked the sweatshirt much more than the guy, so I'd kept it.

What I wasn't wearing, however, was a bra or underwear. Rosemarie hadn't had time to wait for those niceties. She'd needed donuts. I'd barely had time to slip my feet into black UGGs (without socks) and the down-quilted, black coat I'd gotten on sale at Eddie Bauer. My hair had been damp, so I'd braided it and pulled a hot pink, wool watch cap down over my ears. My face was scrubbed clean, and if I'd been buying booze instead of donuts I would've gotten carded for sure.

In other words, I didn't look my best. And Nick always looked amazing. He was movie star handsome, with dark hair, swarthy skin, and the kind of bones that only came from someone of good breeding. His eyes were the color of arctic waters, and every time he took his clothes off I wanted to jump his bones. Fortunately, he liked having his bones jumped. Otherwise, I'd probably be in jail for sexual harassment.

His entire family was filthy rich and his grand-father was a senator. And other than his grandfather, I'd never met people more awful than Nick's family. Someday they'd be giving Satan tips on how to run hell.

I kept my gaze straight ahead. "Help yourself," I said, blindly handing him the almost-empty box.

I stared at the inside of the car door, and fo-cused on keeping my breathing steady. I was afraid if I turned around and looked at him it would be like staring at the sun and I might go blind.

I hadn't been expecting Nick to arrive at the scene. He was homicide. And it seemed like someone was always getting murdered in Savannah, so it was a pretty full-time job.

"What are you doing here?" I somehow managed to sound nonchalant, even though it felt like there was a frog in my throat.

"I caught a double last night. I was just heading home when I heard the call come in. And then I saw Rosemarie's car and my Spidey-sense started tingling."

"It could've been anyone's car," I said. "I'm sure dozens of people drive yellow Beetles in this city."

I could practically feel his shrug. "Perhaps. But not all of them decorate the headlights with big eyelashes or have vanity plates that say HT4TCHR."

I couldn't argue with that. Rosemarie wasn't known for her subtlety.

"So what's the situation?" he asked.

I was being an idiot. I couldn't keep hiding behind the car door and not face him. I was a grown woman. And my legs had fallen asleep.

"We were just passing by," I said, hoisting myself out of the crouch I was in. I bit my lip to keep from whimpering and half dragged myself back into the passenger seat, rubbing the stinging needles out of my legs. "Just another day in the life of me. Several shots were fired and it turns out my Aunt Scarlet is inside."

"Is she the one who was in the OSS and killed all her husbands?" he asked.

"Yes to the OSS," I said. "She probably didn't kill her husbands. At least on purpose. Probably being married to her is enough to kill any man."

"The women in your family are hell on men," Nick said.

That was pretty much the truth. Scarlet had outlived five husbands, my mother had outlived my father, and my sister Phoebe chewed men up and spit them out on a regular basis. And come to think of it, I wasn't doing so hot either. I'd never been married, but I'd accidentally hit my ex-fiancé with my car. It turned out he'd been poisoned before he ran in front of me, so technically I didn't kill him.

I finally looked up and wished I hadn't. Nick looked terrible. His face was gaunt, and a couple days growth of beard covered his face. His slacks and dress shirt were wrinkled and he'd taken his tie off somewhere along the way, so his collar was open and his undershirt peeked through. He hadn't even bothered with a coat, though it was almost freezing outside and little puffs of white fog escaped his mouth. His hair was a little longer since I'd last seen him, but he worked so much there was never time to get it cut. His expression was grim. The double he'd caught must've been a bad one.

"You okay?" I asked.

"I've been better. You ever meet Rick Chandler? He was a sergeant out of patrol."

"Never heard of him." And then I caught on. "*Was?*"

Nick's eyes went cold as ice and he nodded. "A neighbor heard shots and called 9-1-1. At first glance it looks like a murder/suicide. Chandler and his wife have been on the rocks for more than a year now. He had a girlfriend and the wife wasn't too happy about it."

"I can imagine," I said, brows raised. "Wives are weird like that. So she offed him and turned the gun on herself?"

"Nope, other way around. Only problem is, Chandler was a lefty. And though we train to shoot with both hands, Chandler could only shoot with his left, because he broke most of the bones in his right hand about a decade ago. His trigger finger didn't bend. Guess which hand the gun was found in?"

"I'm going to go with the right."

"There you have it," he said. "We're looking hard, but nothing has come up so far. I figured an armed robbery at the gas station might clear my mind."

"Something only a cop would say."

"I'm starting to think it might have been a rash decision. I've never seen your Aunt Scarlet, but am I right to presume she's the one in the fur coat facing off with the gunman like Dirty Harry?"

I sighed. "Yep, that's her. She's supposed to be on a single's cruise in Italy, so I'm not sure what she's still doing in Savannah."

I was trying to act cool, but in truth my stomach was in knots and a ball of fear was lodged in my throat. Despite her eccentricities, I loved Scarlet. I wanted to be just like her when I was ninety. I was pretty good at holding things together during a crisis. I'd really never had a choice in my family. Between my mother and my sister, there was enough drama to go around, and I was always the one left to be the responsible adult.

Which was terrifying if you thought about it. I was thirty years old—thirty-one in another week—and just starting to get my shit together.

"Are you doing okay?" Nick asked. "You look a little pale."

"I'm good. The gunshots worried me a bit, but Scarlet is still standing. She's actually got a musket ball lodged in her hip. One of her husbands collected antique weapons and it misfired. Though Scarlet likes to tell everyone he shot her on purpose."

"She seems like a handful," Nick said. "Must run in the family. By the way, does your Aunt Scarlet carry a big silver revolver in her purse?" Nick squinted. "Looks like a .44."

Rosemarie and I both shot up to a standing position and watched in horror as Scarlet held the revolver in a two-handed grip, right at the robber's mid-section. They were in a standoff, and I figured the gun weighed almost as much as Scarlet. I watched in fascination as the expression on the robber's face changed and he started shaking his head. I couldn't hear what she was saying, but I didn't have to, to know that Scarlet was reading him the riot act. She was mean as a snake when she wanted to be.

The robber backed up a few steps, but didn't lower his gun. That was his mistake. The *crack* from the revolver made me flinch and I heard gasps—including my own—as she fired point blank at the robber. The only problem was, the revolver kicked like a mule and the recoil adjusted her aim upward several inches. The gun thwacked her in the head and Scarlet went down for the count.

A high-pitched scream was heard from inside and the robber came running out, one hand holding up the gun in surrender and the other pressed against his ear.

"Crazy bitch!" he yelled, his voice a couple octaves higher than normal. "Fuckin' bitch shot my ear off. What the hell is the wrong with the old people in this city?"

Police cars had swarmed in around us and they all held their weapons on the robber, demanding he get down on the ground, while he danced around in pain.

Hostages started filing out the front door, looking a little dazed, but there was no Scarlet, so I started toward the door. Despite the fact that she always seemed larger than life and scary as hell, she was still a ninety-year-old woman.

But before I could get there Scarlet stumbled out the front door, her giant handbag hanging over one arm, the other wrapped around a very attractive man who was at least fifty years younger than she was. There was a knot the size of a goose egg right in the middle of her forehead, and bruising was already forming around her eyes, making her look like a raccoon. The gun was nowhere in sight. Probably for the best.

"You're going to need another box of donuts," Nick said. "She looks like she could use a few."

"It feels a little weird standing and talking like this. Like everything is normal."

"Everything *is* normal. I love you and you love me. You're just being a stubborn dummy. And stop avoiding me. It's not like I'm going to re-ask you to marry me every time we're in the general vicinity. I've missed seeing you."

I sighed as that clawing feel of panic started rising up inside me, just like it had the first time I'd been left at the altar. And then a wave of sadness washed over me. "I've missed seeing you too," I finally said. "A lot."

"That makes me feel better," Nick said, grinning for the first time that morning. "Serves you right. Clock's ticking, Addison. Your month is almost over. You're going to have to give me an answer soon."

My eyes narrowed and my hands went to my hips. "I know what damned day it is," I said.

"Good, because the second your time is up I'm taking the tracker off my car. I can promise you won't see me coming."

He grasped hold of my arms and pulled me into him for a hard, fast kiss. I might have melted against him a little too long. It was hard to be sure because he'd scrambled my neurons, and I was wishing desperately I'd taken the time to put on underwear that morning.

I vaguely heard Aunt Scarlet somewhere in the background telling her rescuer she wanted him to meet her niece. I assumed she was talking about me, and I rolled my eyes before I could help it.

Nick grinned and let me go. "See you around," he said, whistling as he headed back to his truck.

"Maybe I need to forget about looking for men at assisted living," Rosemarie said. "Maybe I should hang out at the police station more."

"Statistically, cops don't make the best husbands," I said, frowning. Though I knew several who'd been able to make it work.

"That's okay. I'm thinking I might still be in the rebound stage before I find *the one*. I hear cops are excellent rebounders. Plus, they carry all kinds of interesting things on their belts. Like handcuffs and those little leather paddles."

"The only cops that carry little leather paddles are the ones at Chippendales. Real cops aren't into spanking while making an arrest."

"That's a shame," she said. "Seems like it would make things more interesting."

CHAPTER TWO

THE EMTS WANTED to check Scarlet out, or at least have her stop by the emergency room on the way back home. Scarlet declined. I wasn't so sure that was the best idea, considering the bump on her forehead looked as if she was giving birth to an alien creature. But I had to hand it to her hair dresser. The white helmet hadn't budged an inch.

We piled Scarlet, her fur coat, and her loaded handbag into the back of Rosemarie's Beetle. About halfway back to the office Scarlet started looking like her eggs had been scrambled pretty good, so we swung through Dairy Queen and grabbed her a hot fudge sundae. When donuts didn't work, it was always smart to go with ice cream.

"What are you doing in Savannah?" I asked her. "I thought you were going on that single's cruise to Italy."

"It turns out they have an age limit. Can you believe that? They told me I'd have to go on a senior's cruise. I asked them how I was supposed to be a cougar on a senior's cruise, but they didn't budge an inch. I've been thinking about buying the cruise ship and firing the whole lot of them."

Aunt Scarlet was richer than Croesus. No one's really sure how she came by her money, but knowing Scarlet, it was probably an interesting story. She'd been sent to France at the tender age of seventeen for seducing two of Whiskey Bayou's most prominent businessmen. They'd both been married at the time, but apparently they'd been prepared to leave their wives for Scarlet. They'd actually challenged each other to a duel, and there'd been an exchange of gunfire.

Scarlet hadn't really been interested in either of the men, so she'd traveled to France to live with a distant cousin when the scandal broke. That's where she'd been recruited by the OSS. She'd always said the years she spent as a spy were the best of her life. Even at seventeen, she'd been sneaky as hell and an expert at getting men to tell her secrets once the lights went out.

"You don't happen to have any of that

Percocet in your purse, do you?" she asked. "I sure could use some. My head's pounding. That gun really has a kick."

"I don't typically carry prescription drugs in my purse to sell on the open market."

"Oh, right. You're the good one. Where's your sister? She's always got something. That medical marijuana is something else. Cures all kinds of stuff. I'm probably going to live another twenty-five or thirty years."

"I've got Tylenol," I said. "And Kate has a bottle of whiskey in her desk drawer at the office."

"That'll work," Scarlet said.

"You've never shot that gun before?" Rose-marie asked.

"Oh, sure. Shot a hole right in the floor of the detective agency just last week."

"It's probably best you don't remind Kate about that," I told Scarlet. "She was pretty mad. Those are original hardwood floors."

"No they're not," Scarlet said. "That building burned to the ground when I was a young girl. Took that whole side of the block down with it. It was the original building for the Savannah Morning News, and some lunatic tossed his cigarette on top of a stack of freshly printed newspapers. Whole thing went up like a tinderbox. The building y'all are in isn't even a hundred years old. Besides, a bullet hole in the floor gives a place character. I've had bullet holes in almost all my homes."

"Those are pretty big bullets," Rosemarie said. "I once shot a .44 at a piñata at my cousin's fortieth birthday party and the bullet went through the piñata and the side of the house. When we went in to see how much damage it had done, we found a hole in every wall. It went clear out the other side. Never did find where it ended up."

Scarlet nodded. "They pack a wallop. I think I need something smaller. Back in my day, I carried a lovely pearl-handled revolver that fit in my evening bag. And I always had a stiletto in my garter. I've had to be more creative as I've gotten older. I don't wear garters anymore. They fall right to my ankles, and that's no good when you've got a knife in there. Stabbed myself right in the foot once. Had to get ten stitches."

Scarlet leaned back in the seat and propped her white sneaker on the console between me and Rosemarie. And then she hit her heel against the flat surface and a blade shot from the toe of her sneakers.

"Holy shit," Rosemarie said, swerving off the road and driving up on the curb. The car behind her blared his horn and then passed us, flipping us the bird for good measure.

I stared wide-eyed at the knife that had popped up just a few inches from my face and swallowed hard. "Didn't see that one coming," I said.

"That's the whole idea," Scarlet said. "I'm a dangerous old lady. People underestimate me all the time."

"How do you get it back in?" Rosemarie asked.

Scarlet clucked her tongue. "That's the tricky part. You gotta push it back in. It's easier to do if you take the shoe off first. I learned that the hard way. Was a time when I first got them that I felt just like Johnny Depp in that movie."

"*Edward Scissorhands?*" I asked.

"No, *Sweeney Todd*," Scarlet said, looking thoughtful. "But that one works too. Johnny has a movie for every occasion. He's like Hallmark."

She waggled her foot in my direction and I leaned away from the blade. "Addison, just pull the whole thing off."

I carefully pulled her shoe off and passed it

back to her so she could retract the blade, and she passed me her empty sundae container in trade.

"I don't feel so good," Rosemarie said. "I think I need some Tums. And maybe a nap."

She turned onto State Street, and there wasn't a parking spot to be found. The McClean Detective Agency sat on the corner in a three-story brick building with ivy rioting up the side. The front windows looked out across Telfair Square. The park was still green, though sparser than it was in the spring and summer.

Directly across the agency was the bank, to the right of the square were two federal buildings, and to the left of the square was the Trinity United Methodist Church. It was an upscale area, and my best friend and owner of the agency, Kate McClean, was no dummy when it came to knowing where the higher-end clients would be. She had five full-time private investigators working for her, including me, and a few cops that worked details for her when needed. She also had Lucy Kim, who was the gatekeeper at the front desk. I got paid a percentage of the fee once I solved a case, and so far, I could almost pay all of the bills that had been past due back when my life had started spiraling down the toilet.

"You can just drop us off," I told Rosemarie. "It'll be impossible to find close parking. Too many tourists out and about."

"I don't know what these people are doing here in January anyway," Scarlet said, her shoe firmly back in place. "Why the hell anyone would come here in January just to buy homemade soaps and eat corn pudding that has three-thousand calories in it is beyond me. I'd rather be on a beach drinking Mai Tais."

"We can always go back to the nudist colony," Rosemarie said.

"No we can't," I butted in. "They kicked us out. They said we're not Hidden Sunrise material. Apparently it upset the other guests when the FBI showed up wearing clothes to make an arrest."

"Just as well," Scarlet said. "I had so much sand up my hoo-ha I'm surprised I wasn't making pearls."

Rosemarie and I both curled our lips in disgust, and I thought I saw Rosemarie gag a little. Her face was tinged green and she was a little clammy. She pulled in front of the agency and I got out and leaned the seat forward to help Scarlet.

"You don't look so good," I told Rosemarie, leaning back in.

"She just needs to chuck it up," Scarlet said, leaning in next to me. "She'll feel right as rain after that. Drink a little castor oil and you'll be throwing up your toenails lickety-split."

Beads of perspiration dotted Rosemarie's upper lip and her hands gripped the wheel. "I'll be fine. I just need a nap and a *Dancing with the Stars* marathon. I'll see y'all later."

We watched as Rosemarie sped away and barely missed a few pedestrians in the crosswalk.

Scarlet clucked her tongue. "She won't make it another block before she's decorating the street. Damned embarrassing. Back in my day a woman knew how to keep her donuts down."

I wasn't exactly sure what that meant, but I knew from experience it was never a good idea to argue with Scarlet, so I *hmmmed* appropriately and helped her up the steps to the agency.

"I think we need to get some ice on your forehead," I said. "I really wish you'd let me take you to the hospital to have you checked out."

"No way," she said. "I'm an old lady. Once you take an old lady to the hospital they never let you leave. They're always doing tests and sticking tubes up your butt to see what your colon looks like. Doctors are fascinated by old people's colons and bowel movements. I think it's unnatural. I haven't had anyone interested in my colon since my second husband, and that's just because he was secretly gay. The man was beautiful to look at, but didn't know what the hell to do with a vagina. One time he was down there and burst into tears. He died before we could get an annulment. Rest his soul," she said, making another sign of the cross.

"Okay," I said, brightly. "No doctor. But when we get inside you're going to rest and let us take care of you. You look like you got in a fight with a heavyweight. And lost."

"I wouldn't mind some ice, but drugs would be better."

"I'll see what I can do."

I WAS RELIEVED to see Lucy wasn't at her desk.

There was something about Lucy Kim that scared the ever-loving daylights out of me. She was just a couple inches over five-feet, but she always wore pencil-thin heels that added an extra four inches. Her hair was like black silk and fell straight as rain to the center of her back, and her eyes were as black as her heart. Okay, maybe I made up that last part. I had no clue if she even had a heart. At least a beating one. The most workable theory I had was that Lucy was a vampire, though I hadn't worked out how she walked around in the daytime without turning to ash.

I'd never heard her speak, and I'd never seen her eat or drink anything. Lucy was an enigma. But I was pretty sure she knew a hundred ways to kill a man and never get caught. And I was almost positive her role in the detective agency wasn't just a secretary. I hadn't heard any news reports of vigilantes roaming the streets of Savannah at night, but if I had, Lucy would be my first choice.

"It feels like old people in here," Scarlet said as I led her toward Kate's office. "Depressing as hell."

"I'm sure Kate will be glad to hear that. Maybe you mean old money," I said. "Everything is very tasteful. It's a business. She can't have those paintings of blue dogs hanging up everywhere."

"I don't see why not. Those suckers are expensive. Got two of 'em hanging in my bathroom."

She wobbled a little and I grabbed her elbow for support. "Besides, I know exactly what I'm talking about. I'm old and I've got old money. I never liked the snooty rich people who liked this kind of stuff. I've got trains in my attic. Have I ever shown them to you?"

The change of subject took me by surprise, but I rolled with it. "You've never invited me to your house. I don't even know what state you live in."

"It's better that way," Scarlet said. "That way if you're ever captured and tortured you won't be able to give them the information they're looking for."

I knocked on Kate's door wondering what kind of secrets Scarlet might be keeping that someone would want to kidnap her family for. It was better not to think about it.

"Come in," Kate called out.

Kate and I had been best friends since diapers. I always thought of her as a tiny titan. She was constant motion in a five-foot-two package, and she was cute as a button. Her face was always free of makeup, her dark blonde hair was cut in a no-nonsense chin-length shag, and she never wore anything but black, brown, or gray boxy suits to work, much to my dismay.

She'd been a cop for a couple of years before she decided the politics and bullshit weren't for her, but she'd made enough contacts to get the P.I. business started and build a solid clientele. Kate was as practical as they came, and she'd always been a voice of reason through the years. I liked to think I balanced her out a little so she wasn't all work and no play, but mostly I gave her heartburn.

"Holy cow," Kate said when she looked up from the files on her desk. "What happened?"

"I shot his ear clean off," Scarlet said. "Do you have any of that medicinal marijuana? I've got a bit of a headache."

"No kidding," Kate said. "You've got a mountain growing out of the center of your forehead."

Kate dug through the bottom drawer of her desk while I led Scarlet to the brown leather sofa in the little sitting room attached to the office. It was a large space that Kate used to interview potential clients and feed them coffee and cookies until they paid their retainer fees.

I got Scarlet settled and covered her with a blanket, and Kate called Lucy at the front desk to ask for a couple of ice packs.

"I'm fresh out of medicinal marijuana, but I've got Vicodin," Kate said.

"That'll do. I don't have any Cheetos anyway."

Kate handed Scarlet the drugs and a bottle of water, and we both watched as she swallowed them and laid back on the couch. Lucy entered and handed us an ice pack, and then she left as silently as she came.

"There's something unnatural about that girl," Scarlet said, nodding toward Lucy after she'd left. "I knew someone like that during my days as a spy. She never said a word. Always looked like she was up to something."

"Was she a double agent?" I asked.

"Nope. It turns out she'd lost her tongue in a horrible accident and couldn't speak. And she'd lost an eye in the same accident and it was replaced with a glass eye, which is why she looked so shifty all the time. But that girl there is more than she seems. I bet she's bedded a man or two to get his secrets. Like recognizes like."

"Is it too early to start drinking?" Kate asked me.

"Believe me, alcohol doesn't help," I said, dropping into one of the oversized chairs next to the couch. I already felt like I'd put in a full day.

I was going to have to take responsibility for Scarlet. She was an old woman who was injured. I had no idea where her home was, if she had a car, or if she had someone to take care of her. The only thing I knew with certainty was that I had to keep Scarlet away from my mother. They hated each other with the kind of cold disdain and insults that only Southern women had a talent for.

"Do I want to know whose ear you shot off?" Kate asked.

Scarlet narrowed her eyes. "Armed robber at the gas station. He shot the shit out of their ceiling and scared the bejeezus out of all the poor customers. I couldn't let that stand with my training, so I took him out. Only problem was I forgot what a kick that gun has. Knocked me right on my keister."

"Are you living back in Georgia fulltime?" Kate asked. "I didn't realize you had a conceal carry permit."

"Don't need one," Scarlet said, unconcerned. "I've got a universal pass from my days in the OSS."

"I'm pretty sure that's not how it works," Kate

said. But it was no use. Scarlet was fast asleep. Her hands were crossed over her chest and the only reason I knew she was still alive was because of the gentle snores escaping her mouth.

"How long do you think she's going to stay there?" Kate asked.

"No telling. If we're lucky it'll be a couple of days. Sleeping keeps her out of trouble."

"Right, well I've got an appointment at ten-thirty with a new client. In fact, I need you to be at the meeting. He personally requested you for the job." Kate looked me up and down, taking in my wardrobe choices of that morning. "You still sleeping in your office?"

"Yep."

"By your attire I'm assuming you're not having sex with anyone."

"I'm on sabbatical. Sex with Nick clouds my judgment. I can't make rational decisions when he's naked. That man's a sex wizard."

"So instead of having crazy Hogwart's sex, you're sleeping like a bag lady in your office and wearing clothes that wouldn't tempt a nympho-maniac."

"Stop trying to be logical," I said, closing my

eyes. "I just had to do what felt right. I needed time to think on my decision, and Nick agreed to give me a full month. Didn't you have cold feet when you and Mike got married?"

"No," Kate said. "It's marriage. You either love each other or you don't."

"There are a lot of variables. I don't have the best track record when it comes to marriage."

"Bullshit," Kate said, rolling her eyes. "You don't have the best track record when it comes to *weddings*. Weddings and marriages aren't the same thing. You've never been married, therefore you don't have a track record. And your track record with weddings sucks because you were engaged to a narcissistic gigolo who couldn't keep his dick in his pants. Karma came and bit him in the ass."

I had to agree. Karma had been a real bitch to my ex-fiancé.

"What you need is to skip the wedding this time. Just elope. Then you can overcome the fear you have of finding Nick consummating your vows with someone else."

"I've got exactly seven days to make a decision," I said. "Maybe I should just flip a coin."

"You can't tell me you don't already know

what you're going to tell him. Why are you dragging it out?"

"What's if it's the wrong decision?" I said, throwing my hands up in the air. "I don't need this kind of pressure right now. The stress is affecting me. When I took a shower this morning a clump of my hair came out right in my hand. And I've gained ten pounds since I got my P.I. license."

"You had it to gain," Kate said. "But you probably shouldn't eat a whole box of donuts."

"I only got two," I said dramatically. "Nick and Rosemarie ate the rest. And marriage is a big deal. Why doesn't anyone else understand that but me?"

"Because you're acting like a lunatic. Nick loves you, despite your weirdness. And you love him. Despite the fact that you keep looking for reasons not to. Now go change out of your bag lady clothes and be back here for the ten-thirty. If Nick still seemed interested in marrying you after seeing you dressed like that then you know you have a winner."

I stuck my tongue out at Kate. She didn't see it, but it made me feel better.

CHAPTER THREE

I WAS FEELING a little more stable once I dressed in regular clothes and did something with my hair. I looked at my reflection in the small mirror hanging on the back of my office door and turned my head from side to side. Maybe what I needed was small changes in my life. Like a new hairstyle or color. I'd worn my dark brown hair to the middle of my back since high school. And other than the ill-advised bangs I'd cut myself last year, it hadn't changed much over the years.

I'd pulled on a pair of black leggings and an oversized angora sweater the color of a good merlot. The weather was supposed to turn nasty by nightfall, so I wore my knee-high leather boots and capped the look off by looping an infinity scarf around my neck. This was the south. We accessorized to go to the grocery store. If my mother had seen me in public in what I'd worn this morning she would've had kittens.

Since I'd moved out of Whiskey Bayou and into Savannah, it took a little longer for word of mouth to reach her. My mother's reach was far and wide. And it always seemed like someone was watching. She had spies everywhere.

I was in better spirits since Kate's pep talk, so I swiped on some lipstick the same color as my sweater and grabbed an empty notepad before heading to the conference room.

"Hey, Holmes," Jimmy Royal called out as I passed by.

I stuck my head inside his office and looked around. His space was about five-times the size of mine, which made sense, considering my office had been converted from a janitor's closet. He'd decorated it with a mixture of sports memorabilia and divorced ex-cop. It wasn't a good look. But he was a great P.I.

Jimmy was second-in-command at the agency. He was just over six feet tall and thin as a rail. He lived on Chef Boyardee and Cracker Barrel, and I'd never seen him wear anything on his feet but the same pair of cowboy boots. I had no idea how he walked quietly in those when he was on a case. I made noise walking in my bare feet.

"What's up?" I asked.

"I found a lead on that RV you're looking for. A friend of mine outfits them custom. He said he had a buyer fall through, so he's got one ready for pick up if you want it."

"I don't think I want an RV. Just a van. I'd never be able to park it in the city."

"This is about the size of a van. They still call it an RV if it's got all the junk inside it."

"Oh wow. How far out of my budget is it?"

Jimmy's eyebrows arched into his receding hairline. "Let's just say it's a good thing you caught the Romeo Bandit and received a piece of the reward. You should have enough for both the van and to buy a new outfit and burn whatever you were wearing this morning. I felt my balls draw right up inside my body as soon as I looked at you. So good job on the birth control, if that was your angle."

My eyes narrowed and my mouth tightened at the corners. "Well, thank God," I said. "If your balls had been hanging down like a caveman I'm not sure I'd have been able to resist jumping your bones. I guess the universe is safe from more little

Jimmy's running around. How many child support checks are you writing these days?"

"You're a vicious, mean, devil woman, Addison Holmes. You should've been a cop."

He winked and I took the business card he held out with his friend's information on it. "Thanks, I'll give him a call."

Back when I was teaching, I drove a cherry-red 350Z. But I hadn't been able to afford the payments after I'd lost my job, so I'd sold it to keep my head above water. My last car had a hole in the floorboard the size of a toddler and the brakes hadn't worked so well. And when I say not so well, I mean not at all. It's a miracle I'm still alive.

I'd moved in with Nick shortly after my last car had gone to car heaven, and he'd let me drive the sporty little Audi convertible he used for special occasions. I loved that car. It fit me like a glove and it had been programmed to listen to my voice commands. But because I'm a person of high moral fiber, I'd left the car in the garage and the keys on the hook after the infamous marriage proposal, even though Nick had told me I was more than welcome to keep using it.

I know what you're thinking. Nick is an amazing guy, and I'm an idiot for not dragging that man to the altar. I agree with you. Mostly. But marriage is a big deal. And it's especially a big deal for someone who previously had to tell two-hundred guests that her fiancé was boffing a floozy with bigger boobs and fewer brains in the honeymoon limo. It wasn't one of the high points in my life. In fact, it ranked right up there with wetting my pants on the Jumbotron at a Falcon's game when I'd been in third grade. They'd showed highlights of that for weeks.

The point is, I'm ninety-nine point nine percent sure Nick would never cheat on me. But it was that point one percent that was making me mainline Blue Bell and Tums on a daily basis.

Since I'd left the Audi parked in Nick's garage, I'd been without a vehicle. My mother had loaned me her car when I'd been in a pinch, but she drove an exact replica of the General Lee from the Dukes of Hazzard. It wasn't the best car to go unnoticed in. And it was hell to parallel park in downtown Savannah.

Jimmy Royal had been right about one thing. I'd received a nice fat check for apprehending the Romeo Bandit at the nudist colony last week. The

Romeo Bandit had been wanted for the last seventy years, and the reward money had multiplied. Technically, Scarlet had gotten the bulk of the reward, but she'd promised the agency and myself a nice healthy finder's fee. I'd just deposited my check in the bank the day before.

My first thought had been to use the money to buy a Jeep, but then I started thinking that if I was going to take this job seriously and really be a force to be reckoned with, then I needed to live and breathe being a P.I. Really get in the trenches and be more efficient. The proper vehicle was key.

I started looking at what the other agents all had in common. They were four middle-aged, retired cops with a handful of divorces under their belts, and they were all in pretty good shape. Kate didn't hire slouches with pot bellies. They were a little quirky and a lot cynical. My dad had been a cop in Savannah for thirty years, so I was experienced in dealing with the eccentricities that cops tended to acquire the longer they were on the job. It used to drive my mother crazy that my dad would always back into his parking spot in the driveway. A lot of other things drove her crazy too, but that was a big one. In fact, they mostly drove each other crazy, but I digress.

The difference between the other P.I.'s at the agency and myself, despite the obvious, was that they were outfitted with the proper equipment. They each owned a non-descript van that made the P.I. life more comfortable. There was nothing like being on a stakeout after drinking a Route 44 limeade from Sonic and not a bathroom in sight. The guys' advice had been to carry around a bucket in my car for such emergencies, just so I didn't risk losing my tail if I left to go the bathroom. But there are some things that no Southern woman will ever do. And urinating in a bucket in the back seat of her car is one of those things.

After I'd done a little snooping, I realized that the other P.I.s didn't pee in a bucket either. They all had working toilets, a mini fridge for snacks, and a microwave in their vehicles. Working toilets and snacks were two of my favorite things, so it only made sense for me to get my own van. And now I had the hookup, thanks to Jimmy Royal.

I was early to the conference room, so I helped myself to the coffee and ignored the cookies that sat in the middle of the long conference table. I was turning over a new leaf starting today. I'd be an adult and give Nick an adult decision. And I'd stop stress eating. Unless it was meatloaf or chicken fried steak. Or a strawberry sundae, which had both fruit and dairy, so was probably considered healthy in some medical circles.

I didn't have to wait long. I stood as Kate held open the door for a man who was probably in his late forties or early fifties. He was dressed well—expensive loafers and a tailored shirt and slacks. His hair was blond and parted to one side, making him look a little like a Ken doll. The only difference was this guy was missing Ken's tennis tan and pearly white smile. He was hunched over and moving very slowly. And his face was an odd shade of green and glistened with perspiration, as if every step was a struggle.

If I was a betting woman, I'd say he was an attorney. I hated doing jobs for attorneys. They wanted you to do all the dirty work, and then let you know all the potential lawsuits you might incur if they weren't satisfied with the job. In fact, Kate had turned down several jobs from high profile attorneys because she'd gotten the gut feeling they'd be more trouble than they were worth. Kate's gut feelings were legendary.

But this guy didn't look high profile, at least not at the moment. He looked like he'd been dragged through an alley and left to die. Which made him a little more intriguing, but I was still weary.

"Addison, this is Anthony Dunnegan," Kate said. "He's an attorney with Capshaw, Gates, and Dunnegan."

Ten points for me. I reached out to shake his hand and managed not to grimace when his clammy palm touched mine. "I'm Addison Holmes," I said. "Kate tells me you've got an interesting dilemma."

Anthony inched his way to the conference table and gingerly sat down. He was looking bad enough that I wondered if he shouldn't be in a hospital. I looked at Kate, but she shook her head subtly, reading the look of concern on my face. Kate took the seat at the head of the table and passed a file across to me.

"I'm not sure dilemma is the right word, Ms. Holmes. Someone stole one of my kidneys."

CHAPTER FOUR

"I 'M NOT SURE I understand," I said. "Did you have it in a cooler?"

Generally, when we got theft cases it was jewelry, art, or in one case, an original replica of the Enterprise from Star Trek. This was my first stolen internal organ.

"No," Anthony said. "I had it in my body. They kidnapped me, cut me open, and stole my kidney."

My mouth dropped open and my nose scrunched in horror. "That's terrible. Is this a new thing?" I asked Kate. "I haven't heard of a rash of organ thefts in Savannah." Then I looked back at Anthony. "You're lucky to be alive."

"Believe me, when I woke after the anesthesia wore off, I wished I was dead. I don't have time for violations of my rights such as this. I'm a very busy man. I want you to find the bastards that did this to me and I'm going to destroy each and every one of them."

"And stop them from doing this to other people as well," I said with my Southern smile. The one that was all teeth and no substance. "You'll be a real hero."

I must've been laying it on too thick because Kate took the reins. "Why don't you start at the beginning. When did this happen?"

"A week ago yesterday," he said. "I had a business dinner at The Olde Pink House at six. My clients left a little after seven, and I wasn't quite ready to go home yet."

"That's not a very long business dinner," I said. "Hardly time to get your food and eat."

"They had cocktails and appetizers," he said, giving me a look that said I was being a little impertinent. I got that look a lot. "If you must know, I've been facilitating a merger between their company and another for the last two years. It's very delicate work with a lot of pieces to the puzzle. And they decided they no longer want to go through with the merger. Which as I tried to explain to them, was probably going to get them sued. They'd signed a contract and taken money in good faith. Needless to say, they weren't happy with my advice and dinner was cut short."

He twisted his wedding band on his finger over and over again, a nervous gesture that didn't go unnoticed. He cleared his throat. "With my appetite gone, I moved over to the bar. I had a couple more drinks, and that's when this woman sat next to me. She didn't talk to me. Or even look at me, for that matter. But she was one of those women who command attention. I've never seen anyone more beautiful, and I've been with a *lot* of women."

My dislike for Anthony Dunnegan was growing by leaps and bounds. "Did you strike up a conversation with her?" I asked.

He leaned back in the conference chair and winced in pain. I was assuming it was from his lack of kidney and not his lack of conscience.

"No, but I slipped my wedding ring off and put it in my pocket, just in case."

He said it so nonchalantly it took my brain a second to catch up. I was guessing putting his wedding ring in his pocket "just in case" was a pretty common occurrence.

We had all kinds of clients at the McClean Detective Agency. Some of them were the ones being wronged. And sometimes the clients were the ones doing wrong and they just wanted to cover their bases out of sheer paranoia. I'd come to understand why cops didn't trust anyone. Everyone lied or shaded the truth. About everything.

Kate always said it wasn't our job to judge, only to do the job we were hired for. I thought that was a big bunch of baloney since this was the South and our favorite pastime was judging. Silently, of course. We weren't heathens.

"Anyway, this woman strutted up to the bar like she owned it, and shrugged off her fur coat. That sure as hell got everyone's attention. She was wearing this black dress." He got a glassy look in his eyes as he brought it back to mind. "It shouldn't have been a showstopper, because it was long sleeved and stopped just above her knees. She was very voluptuous." He motioned with his hands. "Like Sofia Vergara. But without the accent. And she had blue eyes. Actually, maybe she looked more like Wonder Woman."

"I'm sorry," I said, stopping in my note taking. "Wonder Woman?" I was thinking maybe Anthony Dunnegan was on some heavy drugs. I still didn't like him, but drugs was a better excuse that plain old asshole.

"Not in costume or anything. That would be ridiculous." He looked at me as if I was the moron in the room. "Like Wonder Woman in her disguise."

"Right. Which Wonder Woman? Linda Carter or Gal Gadot?" I asked. And when Anthony and Kate both stared at me blankly it was me who gave them the disbelieving look. "It's an important distinction for identifying her. 1970s Wonder Woman or today's Wonder Woman? They're close, but there are differences. How am I going to find this woman if I can't recognize her?"

"I did some research on you, Ms. Holmes," Anthony said.

He was trying to intimidate me, but I'd taught history to a bunch of teenagers. Anthony Dunnegan wasn't even in the same ballpark as far as intimidation.

"Okay," I said, unimpressed.

"You've got an impressive record in the short time you've worked here. And you're younger and more enthusiastic…hungrier," he said, giving me a shark's smile, "than the other agents. You seem to get by on a combination of luck and determination, though it's nice you're trying to better yourself by taking classes. Your scores at the firing range were impressive."

"Thank you," I said drolly. "Bettering myself is a top priority of mine. I've found my Master's degree really comes in handy while investigating lowlifes."

His smile widened—a politician's smile—but his eyes were mean. "You've also got a smart mouth and haven't really learned your place."

"My place?" I asked.

"Yes, your place when it comes to who is working for whom. And of course, I heard all about how you embarrassed yourself at Charles and Nina Dempsey's home. Charles and I have been great friends since college."

"That explains a lot," I said.

"I even heard their son called off his engagement to you because of the incident. People like you will never belong in that world. But I've found you do an excellent job getting the dirty work done if the right carrot is dangled in front of your face."

I narrowed my eyes. His green pallor and

sheen of sweat had thrown me off my game. I was usually pretty good at reading people. And I'd taken his sickness as a sign of weakness, and I'd felt automatic sympathy at his situation. But I could see crystal-clear now. And one thing was for certain. Anthony Dunnegan was a snake. And I sure as heck didn't want to work for him.

I scooted my chair back to get up, but Kate put a hand on my arm to stop me. I saw Anthony's vicious grin and knew he thought I was going to be reprimanded.

Kate interrupted before I could say anything that would probably get us sued. "You've received the references of this agency, Mr. Dunnegan. We only employee the best. Our client list is selective. Very selective. I took you on due to a referral from Craig Capshaw, who is an exemplary client of this agency. But if you're going to be a hindrance to my agency and my agents, then you're welcome to go elsewhere. You're hiring us to do a job as we see fit, as you'll remember from the contract you signed. You'll not give orders or interfere in how we run our cases. I can promise that you won't wiggle your way out of the penalties of the contract you signed, as it was drawn up by Mr. Capshaw himself, the senior partner at your firm, I believe."

It was everything I could do to keep the grin off my face and continue looking stern. I was mostly one of those people whose every thought flashed across my face. I'd gotten a lot better at it over the last several months, but I had to concentrate really hard. Kate always told me I looked constipated.

"We've got more than enough business on our plates at the moment. We don't cater to taunts or tantrums. We don't need you. You need us. And we're the best. You already know that. You won't find anyone else who will touch this case. Unless you want to take my original advice and go to the police."

That was an interesting tidbit of information, I thought. The police would be the first place I'd go if I'd woken up in a similar situation.

Color flushed into Anthony's face and I thought anger made him look a little healthier. Though it probably wasn't so good for his blood pressure.

Kate and I waited him out while he got his temper under control. I'd learned a few things after I'd stopped teaching. Teaching was insular. There was a social sphere of protection, especially for women. Things were totally different outside of that sphere of protection.

I had great respect for women who worked in a man's world. Which was essentially what I'd been thrown into when I'd started working for the agency. I was an attractive, intelligent woman with a good education (I had plenty of faults too, but I didn't want to delve too deep into those), but there were still times when I had to turn on the Southern charm to get what I wanted. Being direct didn't work. Not in this part of the country, where men still had definite ideas of a woman's place. If you were direct in the wrong circles that's when you got called a bitch, or pushy and opinionated. So I'd mostly taken my mother's advice and learned to catch more flies with honey than vinegar. But sometimes I wanted to napalm those flies and watch them burn into tiny balls of ash.

I wasn't going to waste my Southern charm on Anthony Dunnegan. It had already been a long day, and I wasn't in the mood to placate a man who clearly wanted to put me and Kate in a position where it looked like we needed his business. I was intrigued by the missing kidney.

But my curiosity would only go so far. And Kate was nobody's pushover. She'd been a badass cop. And she scared the crap out of me when she got a certain look in her eyes. She had that look now, and the green in Anthony Dunnegan's face was starting to make a reappearance.

We sat in a silent showdown for several minutes. I didn't do well with silence. It made me antsy. Which is probably not the best quality for a private investigator to have. Long stakeouts were like torture for me. I normally filled my time by doing crosswords or trying to teach myself how to knit. I'd found a pattern on Pinterest that looked simple, but I showed it to Kate and she'd started laughing until tears fell down her cheeks. How was I supposed to know it was a penis sock? Who even thought of such a thing? This was Georgia, for Pete's sake, not the arctic tundra. No man needed to keep his penis that warm in this climate. But it had been easy to knit, so I'd done several of them in different colors. I'd given them as Christmas gifts to the other agents in the office.

I stared at the plate of cookies for a few seconds, debating whether or not it would make us look weak if I grabbed one and shoved it in my mouth. The seconds ticked by with exaggerated slowness.

And then Anthony started talking as if nothing had happened. "She looked more like Gal Gadot. And now that I think about it, she kind of looked like you too," he said, pointing at me. "But sexier. You're too cute to have that kind of impact. And it's hard to see your body in that baggy sweater, but your legs looked good when I came in, so I'm guessing you're maybe a seven and a half in the body department. Maybe an eight plus if you fixed yourself up a little."

"Thank you," I said dryly.

"Maybe you should think about doing up your eyes a bit. Smudging them at the corners like those models in the Victoria's Secret catalogs. Now that I look at you closer, you could probably be a ten with the right makeup."

"I'll take it under advisement."

"I need to take my pain meds," Anthony said. "I need some water."

Kate got up and brought him back a bottled water from the mini-fridge, and we watched as he pulled a prescription bottle out of his shirt pocket and popped a little white pill in his mouth.

"Are you going to be able to drive home?" Kate asked.

"I'm good," he said. "I've never gotten pulled over for a DWI before. This stuff hardly even affects me anymore. Gotta take double to take the edge off."

Anthony Dunnegan was a horrible and selfish man. I didn't normally wish people ill, but I was starting to think him losing a kidney was just karma coming back to haunt him.

"I ordered a third gin and tonic and said fuck it. Drinking was the best option I had at that moment. I really didn't want to go home, so I figured it wouldn't be too hard to find a place to sleep it off. If I didn't end up leaving with the woman beside me then I could make my way to River Street to find a hotel."

"So how did you go from a third gin and tonic to missing a kidney?" I asked.

"The woman ordered a whiskey and made herself comfortable on the barstool. This woman was class. And she had money. You see a lot of women pretend to have money when they're out trolling, so they fool guys like me that have money into picking them up for the night. And then they rob you blind."

I almost asked if he'd had that experience before, but Kate squeezed my thigh. Hard.

"I figured she was either married to or involved
with somebody who had the kind of job that
might keep them after hours. Like a doctor or
politician. And they stood her up for the night.
She wasn't looking around, scoping out anyone
she might be interested in at the bar, so I was
thinking maybe she actually enjoyed being in a
relationship. She seemed preoccupied, and she
kept checking her watch. A Rolex. I was going to
offer to buy her a drink, but she didn't even glance
my way. I don't want to brag, but I can usually get
the most monogamous woman to stray. I'll admit,
her disinterest stung. I'm an attractive guy. At least
a solid nine, though this surgery has knocked me
down to a six for the time being. And I'm rich."
He held up his own Rolex and pointed to it, just
to make sure we saw it, I guess.

"Besides, she wouldn't have dressed like that if
she didn't want to be noticed."

I was starting to get an eye twitch. I could not
help this man. He was a horrible human being.
Not only was he willing to cheat on his wife, but

he was one of those men who thought women deserved what they got if they dressed too sexy. I'd about reached my limit with Anthony Dunnegan.

I squeezed Kate hard on the knee like she'd done to mine. I needed to get out of here. I needed to go back to my office and lay down on the little memory foam mattress I'd squeezed between the two walls. I wasn't proud of my living arrangements at the moment, but it beat the hell out of living with my mother.

I also needed a fucking cookie, so I snatched one off the table and bit into it, thinking I'd turn over a new leaf tomorrow. Tomorrow was Sunday—the Lord's day. And everyone knew it was easier to stick with dieting commitments when the weight of church guilt was pressing on your shoulders.

I was drawing little caricatures of Anthony Dunnegan on my notepad. My favorite was the one where he was holding his own head. The image was a little dark for me, but it immediately made me feel better. Or that might have been the cookie.

Anthony continued his disgusting tale. "We just sat in silence for a while, drinking away our miseries, and all of a sudden she turns to me and says, 'Want to get out of here?'"

"Did you introduce yourselves?" I asked. "Get her name?"

"I didn't care what her name was," he said, as if I was a moron for even asking. "I cared that she was hot and that she wouldn't be yapping in my ear about how she wants a new Porsche because Jennifer's husband gave her one for her birthday."

I might have actually growled low in my throat, but I kept taking notes. I was going to give the people that stole this guy's kidney a medal when I found them.

"What time did you leave the bar?" Kate asked.

"About ten-thirty. I helped her on with her coat and I paid our tabs."

"That was real gentlemanly of you," I said.

Anthony stared at me, trying to decide if I was making fun of him or not. I was. But sometimes my sarcasm was really subtle.

"You said you were in walking distance of some hotels?" Kate prompted. "Where'd you go?"

"Things get hazy at that point. I was pretty hammered, and she wasn't too steady either. There was a long line for cabs, but there were a few pedi-cabs lined up across the street. I remember it made me laugh. I couldn't imagine a woman like her riding around the city in a pedi-cab. It was ludicrous. But we climbed in, laughing like two horny teenagers."

"Do you remember the pedi-cab company? Or your driver's name? Maybe a description?"

"Are you kidding? I was shitfaced and she had her hand down the front of my pants. I wouldn't have recognized my own mother. All I can tell you is we got in a bright red pedi-cab and our driver was a man. I think. We ended up at another bar. I'm not sure of the name. Charlie's? Chester's? I think it was something like that."

"How long were you in the pedi-cab?" I asked, thinking I could at least get a radius from where they'd started.

"I don't know," he said. "I think I need another pill. It feels like someone set fire to my spine." He popped another pill and chased it with water. "It was a short ride. All I know is that one minute I've got my tongue down her throat and the next I have a case of blue balls that won't quit. I wasn't exactly thrilled about stopping at another bar. But she just laughed and told me she'd make it worth my while. Teasing bitch."

"Yes, focus on that instead of the fact that she probably scammed you for your kidney," I said, shaking my head. Anthony didn't seem to notice. I think his pain pills had started to kick in. He was looking glassy-eyed and a little bit of drool had dripped onto the conference table.

"Do you remember what direction you headed?"

"We were headed toward the river. I think. It could've been the opposite direction. But it wasn't a long ride. She paid the pedi-cab driver and we went into the bar, but I don't remember much about it," he said, shrugging. "The music was loud and it was a real dive. Raina ordered us a couple of martinis and then we danced for a while."

"Wait, who's Raina?" I asked, confused.

"The woman," he slurred. "Aren't you paying attention? That's the name she gave me. It's not her real name, of course. I told her my name was John." His hands were flying in agitation as we struggled to follow his disjointed explanation. "Things got pretty hot and heavy on the dance floor, so we decided to head to the hotel. We took a couple of to-go cups with us. That bar made a damn good martini. Anyway, I was glad we were leaving and getting down to business. I don't always do my best work when I've had a lot to drink, and I wanted to show her a good time."

"I'm sure she was grateful for your thoughtfulness."

"That's what I was thinking too," he agreed, his smile lopsided. "The cab line was long again, so we hopped in another pedi-cab."

"The same one or different this time?" I asked.

"Different. This one was yellow. I only remember that because the color hurt my eyes. It reminded me of Big Bird."

"Which direction did y'all take this time?"

"I'm not sure. Raina just told the guy to start pedaling and she'd let him know where to stop. Things really got hazy after that. Before I knew what was happening she'd crawled up in my lap and I found out firsthand she wasn't wearing any underwear. There's not much you can do in a situation like that except sit back and enjoy the ride, if you know what I mean. She was real discreet too. Used her fur coat to keep us covered. I do remember telling the driver to keep to the darker and less crowded streets. All I needed was one of my clients or a friend of my wife's seeing me. She'd take me to the cleaners in a divorce.

"I can't tell you how long we rode around for or in which directions. That's the best sex I've ever had in my life. And that's pretty much where my memory of the night ends. The next thing I know I'm waking up in a bathtub full of ice and I've got a pounding headache."

"You've got no memories after the sex?" I asked.

"Nothing. I'd literally thought I'd died when I had that orgasm. I saw white lights. I think I maybe took another drink to wet my throat, but it was lights out after that."

"What happened after you woke up in the tub?" Kate asked.

"I had no clue where I was, and my vision was pretty blurry after the anesthesia wore off. I panicked. I knew something was wrong. I couldn't figure out why I was sitting in the ice bath. And then I saw the little tray of surgical instruments sitting by the sink. Freaked the hell out of me. They were clean, but I just had that gut feeling that someone had used them recently. And then I saw the cell phone next to the tray.

"I had no idea who I should call. Not my wife. She'd ask too many questions. My partners at the law firm would ask questions too. The police were out, because if I filed a report and opened an investigation then my wife would find out what'd I'd done all night, and I'd be in a hell of a lot more trouble than I already was sitting in a bathtub full of ice. Then I saw the note on the door."

Anthony visibly shivered and I had a hard time not doing the same. It sounded like something out of a horror story.

"What did it say?" I asked.

"It said if I wanted to live that I needed to call 9-1-1. So that's what I did. I didn't get out of the tub. I didn't do anything. I was too scared. So I called 9-1-1 and sat there and shivered until the manager opened the door for the paramedics."

"You've been in the hospital for a couple of days and you look like hell," I said. "How have you been keeping this from your wife? She's bound to find out."

"I told her I was in Charleston on a business trip. She doesn't really care. The kids are with the nanny and she's taking some extra tennis lessons with her instructor in the Bahamas. I'll be good as new in another week. I told the office I had the flu, so I'm working from home."

"It must be hard to keep all the lies straight," I said.

"Nah, you get used to it. I'm going to lay my head down for a few minutes."

Kate and I watched as he lay his head on the conference table and immediately passed out.

"Mr. Dunnegan," Kate said. "Mr. Dunnegan?" She shook him this time, but he was out. "Dammit, this place is not a hostel for people doped up on pain meds. What the hell am I supposed to do with him?"

In any other situation this would've been funny. But I mostly wanted to drag Anthony Dunnegan by his heels and leave him in the middle of the street.

"Maybe we can shove him in a closet," I said.

"We don't have any closets left. We turned the last one into your office."

"Then I'm out of ideas. What we really need to talk about is this case. Kate, I hate this man. I hope he caught an STD from that woman in the pedicab."

Kate sighed and leaned back in her chair. "I'd

normally agree with you. My first inclination was to turn him down when he called. He's an obnoxious ass, and I can't even imagine what he's like to deal with when he's a hundred percent healthy. But there's a bigger picture here. I did a little digging. Six months ago in Hilton Head, a vacationer was relieved of his heart. He clearly wasn't as lucky as Anthony Dunnegan, but the police report is in your file. There are some similarities, so this isn't necessarily about our current client. This is about the other people out there who are possibly being hunted for their organs. I want you to track these guys down. This is a huge case."

"Then why in heaven's name are you giving it to me? Are you out of your mind?"

Kate smiled and said, "Possibly. But Anthony was right about one thing. You're tenacious and determined. You'll see this through to the end. And you also have solid FBI connections, since this ring will most likely fall into federal territory. Everyone here is on notice to help if you need it, including me. But you have a major talent for getting information from people who don't normally want to give it. You don't look like a cop like the other guys. Read up on the file and start digging."

"Didn't the police have to file a report when Anthony was taken to the hospital by ambulance?"

"The hospital reported it to the police like they were supposed to, but it's the victim's choice whether or not to file a report. He chose not to file one, so the police didn't investigate. A man like Anthony Dunnegan has everything to lose if information leaks about him to the wrong people. He's well acquainted with Nick's parents, and he's got his eye on Nick's grandfather's senate seat when he retires in a couple of years."

"He's not getting my vote. And last I heard, Nick's grandfather isn't planning on retiring. He's still pretty young and in great health."

Nick's grandfather was the only person in Nick's family I liked. He was pretty much the only person in Nick's family that Nick liked too. Nick came from a long line of alcoholics and womanizers on his dad's side, and on his mother's side he came from wealthy debutantes that automatically hated anyone who hadn't inherited family money for the last five generations. I have no idea how Nick turned out so good. His grandfather probably had a lot to do with it.

"I think Nick's parents are pushing the retirement angle. They don't particularly like the senator's politics," Kate said, shrugging. "I guess you won't have to worry about it if you decide not to marry Nick."

"Shut up," I said.

Kate grinned and I took another cookie. "If you keep eating cookies like that you're going to put on a lot more than ten pounds."

"It's the stress. Between the marriage proposal and Aunt Scarlet coming to town, I can't seem to help myself." I wanted to feel sorry for myself and maybe have a good cry, but I didn't really have the motivation at the moment. Mostly I was just tired.

"At least you're not turning to booze and prostitutes," Kate said.

"They have male prostitutes in Savannah?" I asked naively.

"They've got all kinds of prostitutes in Savannah. This town offers a real smorgasbord of sex."

"Huh," I said.

"Let's roll the future senator here into Jorgen's office. He's visiting his daughter in D.C. until next Tuesday."

"How come I never know these things?" I

asked. "I could've been sleeping in his office."

"That's why we have the big calendar in the break room. Maybe check it every once in a while."

"I never go in the break room. Jimmy keeps cooking those frozen burritos in the microwave and they explode. It smells like dirty feet."

"Probably better to sleep in your office anyway. Jorgen likes sardines."

CHAPTER FIVE

W E ROLLED ANTHONY Dunnegan to the end of the hallway and into Harry Jorgen's office. I think it said a lot about the agency that none of the employees even looked twice as we wheeled his office chair down the hall, his head slumped forward on his chest.

I stopped to check on Aunt Scarlet and saw that she was still sleeping peacefully, so I took the file Kate had given me back to my office so I could get better acquainted with it.

My office was at the opposite end of the hall from Kate's, not far from the employee bathroom. It had once been a janitor's closet, but they'd painted the walls a soft neutral and put new carpet down to turn it into an office. I hadn't been able to sit in there for long periods of time after the carpet had been laid because the fumes from the glue made me high, but it was mostly gone now, due to the fact I had three Scentsys plugged in. The office smelled like apple pies, which might have been a contributing factor to my constant hunger.

It had one small desk and a chair, my laptop, a printer, and a floor lamp with an animal print shade that I'd gotten on sale at Pier One. I'd put a round shag rug on the floor in bright red to make the space seem more personable. Shoved against the opposite wall was the thin memory foam mattress I'd miraculously squeezed into the space, covered with Laura Ashley sheets. A rolling suitcase with as many clothes as I could fit into it sat against the wall. It was pathetic.

But it beat the heck out of living with my mother. She was newly married and the walls at Casa de Holmes were a lot thinner than a grown daughter could handle. I'd never had that problem as a child. Apparently my parents hadn't had a very active sex life.

I squeezed behind my desk and opened my laptop, booting it up so I could do some background work. I'd learned my first day on the job that being a P.I. wasn't always excitement and adventure. It was mostly tedious research and backtracking until you stumbled across the thread you were looking for. I was a champ at research, and I actually enjoyed that part of the job.

There was no police report, since Anthony didn't want the cops to pursue the situation, so I went through my notes again. I printed out a map of downtown Savannah and did a search for bars in the area to try to retrace his path. What I did know was that he started the night at the Olde Pink House and ended up eighteen blocks away at a Rest Easy Inn and Suites. And he got there by pedi-cab, unless they'd moved him to a regular cab once he'd passed out.

I also ran a search for bars within three blocks of the Olde Pink House and came across a place named Charlie's. I marked it on the map to pay a visit to, and then opened the police file on the similar crime that had occurred in Hilton Head.

Jonathon Hunt had been a forty-one-year-old man in the prime of his life. He was married with two children and worked as a broker at a top firm in New York before going out on his own. He did even better then. He was a financial genius. He and his family had been on vacation when Jonathon had gone missing. His wife had immediately called the police and filed a report. She'd known something had to be wrong for him to disappear like that. His body was discovered in a hotel three days later by the maid. There was no sign of trauma except for the hole where his heart should've been.

Jonathon's last known whereabouts had been the Shrimp Shack, a restaurant on the water in Hilton Head. The wife said he hadn't been feeling well after a couple of drinks, so he got up to go to the restroom. Witnesses also placed him there. He briefly bumped into a woman who was coming out of the ladies' bathroom, but witnesses said it seemed like he was in a hurry and just moved around her. He went into the bathroom and never came out. He just disappeared.

The autopsy report came back with a minimal dose of Ketamine in his system, as well as traces of GHB. The medical examiner presumed the GHB was used to incapacitate the victim enough to get him moved, and the ketamine was what was used for the surgery, as it was a common anesthetic.

There were contusions around his wrists and ankles, indicating the drug had worn off before the surgery was complete. That, combined with the amount of blood loss arterial bleeding would've caused, led the medical examiner to state the victim had more than likely been awake during the surgery.

I shuddered, thinking of the unbelievable terror Jonathon Hunt must've endured before his death. He'd been awake and aware as his killers took out his heart. And it was killers, plural. The hotel room where Jonathon's body had been found had been spotless at first glance. But blood was hard to clean up, and traces of it had been found with Luminol. They'd had to throw a tarp on the floor and bag all their clothes after the surgery had been done. Most likely anyone in the room would've been covered in blood, especially if the victim had been awake and struggling. The medical examiner made a note that the lack of blood in the body would've been due to the high stress rate of the victim, making blood spurt if they hadn't clamped it off.

It was a surgery that couldn't have been done without medical training, as the autopsy showed that the heart had been removed cleanly.

That was as far as the investigation went. There no weapon, and no suspects. And nothing even remotely similar had been done in the resort community before, so there were no like crimes to compare it to. And just because someone stole a heart six months ago in Hilton Head didn't mean it was the same people who took Anthony Dunnegan's kidney, though my gut was telling me the two crimes were very much related.

I was going to have to take a trip to Hilton Head and do a little investigating of my own. See if any memories had been stirred since some time had passed.

I looked back through the hospital report that Anthony had given to Kate. A mix of Ketamine and GHP had also been found in his system. And it was notated in the chart that the removal of the kidney had been done professionally. He'd been sutured and put on ice to slow his blood flow until the paramedics could rescue him. Anthony and Jonathon also had something else in common. They were both O-negative. And if I remembered right, only a small percentage of the population had O-negative blood.

I did a quick Google search and learned that transplant recipients that had type O blood could only receive transplants from donors that had the same blood type. It was a thread I could tug on later for sure.

My office door banged open and I jumped in surprise. And then I almost screamed when I saw Scarlet standing in the doorway. The swelling on her head had gone down some thanks to the ice, but her face was more colorful than it had been when I'd left her. Her papery thin skin was shades of purple, black, and green, but she'd taken the time to reapply her bright red lipstick, as if that would be a distraction from the rest of her face.

She'd left her fur coat in Kate's office and was wearing a siren-red velour jogging suit that matched her lipstick and the bright white tennis shoes with the hidden knives in the toes. She didn't look altogether sane, but her hair hadn't budged an inch. I was thinking the military should weaponize whatever she used on her hair.

"That medicine Kate gave me was a doozy," Scarlet said. "I feel like a million bucks. It's been seventy years since I haven't felt any aches and pains in my body. Not even the bullet lodged in my hip is paining me today. I need to find a man before it wears off. Think of how good sex would be if you didn't have to worry about pulling a muscle or popping a joint back into place."

"I don't know, Aunt Scarlet. Your face looks like it hurts pretty bad. It's very…colorful."

"It's no wonder you're not married if you think a man cares about what your face looks like when you're horizontal. Not if you're doing it right. I knew a girl in France who was ugly as homemade sin. Best spy I ever met. Men didn't care what she looked like. Taught me a few tricks too," Scarlet said, waggling her eyebrows.

"Or you can just put a bag over your head and a man can pretend you're anyone he wants you to be. That's what I do. The men in my age bracket aren't anything special to look at. Use paper though, not plastic. I once had a lover who liked plastic bags. Come to find out that's a whole different kind of sex. I didn't particularly care for it, but that was back in the seventies, so sexual exploration was a little bit of a grab bag."

"Sweet baby Jesus," I said softly.

"Or you can just turn the lights off. That's probably an easier solution." She came inside my office and looked from side to side. "This here is an embarrassment of an office. I thought you and Kate were best friends."

"I'm a junior agent," I said. "I'm lucky to have an office at all."

"You're a Holmes, and Holmes women don't take crap from anyone, especially their best friends. Sometimes you've got to make demands and not back down. Stare them straight in the eye like a snake charmer."

"Uh, huh," I said. "Kate will love that."

"So what are we doing today?" Scarlet asked. "It's Saturday and I hate being cooped up inside on a Saturday. I know you were sitting here waiting to make sure I was okay, but now that you see I am, I think it's important to get back to work while we still have daylight. I heard the weather is supposed to get real nasty tonight."

"I was actually just working on a new case," I said, the thought of working another case with Scarlet sending a cold knot of fear straight to my belly.

I was almost positive that therapy would never undo the damage of what I'd experienced at the nudist resort.

"Since you're not on the single's cruise, where are you staying?" I asked her.

"I've got a suite over at The Ballastone. They

don't riffle through your things when you're out, so I always stay there. Leave pieces of tape stuck to my drawers just in case though."

"Why don't I take you there so you can get some rest? You probably have a concussion." And then I remembered I didn't have a car and sighed.

"Of course I have a concussion, girl. Did you just fall off the turnip truck? I think being an old maid has made you wonky. I was on my third husband by the time I was your age. Bless their souls. You're going to dry up like a raisin if you're not careful. Best thing you could do is dip your raisin in the ocean and plump it right back up."

"I'm not a hundred percent sure what that means, but I think my raisin is still plump enough, thank you."

I wasn't going to get rid of her. She had that look in her eye I occasionally saw when looking at my own reflection. There was only one way I knew to get her to go rest, and it was playing dirty.

"I need to stop by Mom's. There are still a few of my things there I need to pick up."

Scarlet was silent for a few seconds, her red lips pinched tightly together, and she drummed her fingers on the corner of my desk. I would've hated to play poker with Scarlet. She finally nodded and said, "That's fine. I probably need to pay my respects to your mother anyway. Haven't seen her since your father died. Heard she got remarried. Should probably get her a vase or something. Or maybe her new husband a bottle of whiskey. He'll probably need it."

"Be nice, Aunt Scarlet," I told her.

"I am, I am. Well, let's get going. I'll probably need another one of Kate's magic pills once I see your mother."

"I need to buy a car first," I said, gathering up all the files on my desk and sticking them in my backpack. "I gave Nick's Audi back."

"Well, that was dumb. Who's Nick? Is he hot? Does he have a brother?"

"Nick asked me to marry him. He's Senator Dempsey's grandson."

"Herbert Dempsey?" Scarlet asked, brows raised in surprise. "I knew Herbert's daddy back in the day. And not in the biblical way either. Herbert is good people. His son is a real a-hole though. Hope the grandson isn't. If he is, I can tell you how to get rid of the body without too many questions."

I took a deep breath and grabbed my handbag. "Nick is a lot like his grandfather. He's not an a-hole. He's a cop."

"I always wanted to marry a cop. I hear they're dynamite in the sack."

We headed out the front door of the agency and Lucy was mysteriously gone again. I had a feeling she just wanted to stay out of Scarlet's way. I helped her down the front stairs since her balance was a little off due to the black eyes and her not being able to see all that well, and I hailed a taxi that happened to be passing by.

The cab driver gave a horrified look at Aunt Scarlet and then muttered something under his breath. He was a middle-aged Indian guy with salt-and-pepper hair and bags under his eyes. His name badge clipped to the air vent said Jayesh.

I gave him the address and we mostly rode in silence out of downtown Savannah and across the highway. It wasn't the best part of town. In fact, it was a pretty bad part of town, and I was glad I'd remembered to grab my Glock from the shower caddy. We crossed the highway and Jayesh hit the automatic locks on the doors.

"Don't worry," Scarlet said. "I've got my

sneakers on. And my handbag is loaded."

"Right," I said, thinking that would be the weirdest news story ever. Private investigator and her ninety-year-old aunt gunned down in the projects after buying stolen van filled with snacks and a working toilet.

"Lady, I don't know what business you have here, but it can't be good. I hope you're not expecting me to wait for you."

"No worries, Jayesh. You heard my aunt. She has her sneakers on. I wouldn't want you to do the gentlemanly thing and wait for two women who are in a bad area of town."

"Good," he said, nodding.

"I don't know where chivalry has gone," I said, shaking my head.

"Right in the crapper," Scarlet said.

"Yep," Jayesh said. "This is 2016. Women's lib and all that junk." He came to an abrupt halt on the corner of Graves and Stiles and idled there, hitting the fare button so we could pay our tab.

"Oh, no," I said. "You're not dropping us at the corner. Take us all the way. I'm not walking a half mile down this road in these boots. And look, it's starting to drizzle."

"You're crazy," he said. "Look. Everyone is staring at us. We're sitting targets."

"Time's ticking, Jayesh."

He blew out a sigh and skidded out on the loose rocks in the street. Maybe *street* was being a little too generous. The road wasn't paved and it was half overgrown with weeds. A semi-truck graveyard sat to the left, and a bunch of overgrown trees and weeds taller than the trailer houses grew on the other side.

A couple of Hispanic guys leaned against one of the dead semis, the trailer colorful with graffiti, and stared us down as we passed by. The sky had turned gray and the wind had started to blow. The drizzle was coming a little harder and faster.

"That guy either has a hell of a boner or his gun is bigger than mine," Scarlet whispered. "He better watch out or he'll shoot his pecker right off. Happened to a good friend of mine. Never could pee standing up again. Kept hitting himself right between the eyes."

"Why are you whispering?" I asked.

"It seemed appropriate. Where are we going?"

"A place called Ugly Mo's. He's a car dealer. Kind of."

Jayesh *hmmphed* and drove all the way to the end of the street. It was a dead end. Only one way in and one way out. A couple of metal buildings with peeling paint sat in front of us, and in the parking lot to our right were several rows of cars in various stages of disrepair. It wasn't looking too promising. I was starting to think Jimmy Royal may have set me up big time.

"This is the end of the road, lady," Jayesh said. "Twenty-eight-fifty."

"Hey, at the corner back there it was only eighteen dollars," I said, narrowing my eyes.

"This street's an expensive fare." I handed him thirty bucks and opened the car door.

"What about my tip?" he asked.

"I was going to give you thirty back at the corner. You could've pocketed it but you decided to be a jerk. Now your boss gets the money."

He called me a bitch and put the cab in reverse, speeding back down the road to safety.

"I have a mind to shoot out his tires," Scarlet said. "There's so many laws nowadays. I liked it back when it was an eye for an eye. People these days take offense to every damned thing."

"Especially having their tires shot out," I said.

"Come on. My hair isn't going to last with this weather. Let's go find Ugly Mo."

"I hate to break it to you, but you already look like Troy Polamalu. I'll take you to my salon. You need someone who can tame that hair. If we get out of here alive we should stop by and see if they can squeeze you in."

"I've been thinking of making a drastic change."

"That's your hormones talking. You're not ready to have a baby, so you're needing to change something about yourself. Sometimes I'd get those hormonal urges to have kids. That's when I'd come visit your dad and his brothers. They were the best birth control on the market. Horrible children," she said, shuddering. "And then I'd go buy myself a new pair of shoes or a handbag."

I could kind of understand where Scarlet was coming from with the whole kid thing. I knew I wanted to have kids someday. But I'd spent a good portion of my life in a classroom full of semi-adults that were given a license to operate a car, but didn't know how to balance a checkbook and wrote complete sentences with emojis. It was kind of depressing. And I really liked buying shoes and handbags too.

"Someone has some real artistic talent," Scarlet said. "Wonder if they'd do a wall in my bathroom."

I was assuming Scarlet was referring to the graffiti that covered a good portion of the metal building. There were a lot of creative curse words and a portrait of a scantily clad woman with breasts that defied gravity. Ugly Mo's was written in big block letters in lime green.

"What would you get them to draw on your wall?" I asked curiously.

"That Jason Momoa fella and me and Tom Hardy on one of those heart-shaped beds. I've always been attracted to men that look like they won't break."

"Sometimes I wonder if I'm dead and caught in some kind of horrific purgatory," I said, wondering why I'd asked the question in the first place.

"What's that, dear?"

"Nothing. I don't see anyone. Let's go inside and get out of the rain."

The only door in sight was one of those big garage doors like at a mechanic's shop. There was one fluorescent light hanging from the ceiling, and it smelled like motor oil with a hint of dead animal.

A piece of metal scraped across concrete from somewhere in the darkness of the building. I froze and immediately felt chills crawl across my skin. I glanced at Scarlet to make sure she was okay, and then did a double take. She'd unzipped her jogging suit and was hiding her .44 inside it like an old school gangster, her hand wrapped around the butt of the gun.

"Put that away," I hissed. "You've already been in one shootout today. This is a non-hostile mission. I just want to buy a car, for cripe's sake."

"I've never seen a car lot like this one. What kind of cars do they sell here? Maybe I need a new car."

"Your license got revoked ten years ago," I said. "You can't buy a car."

"I can do whatever I want to. What if I just want to buy a car and look at it? Who's going to stop me? The government. Those bastards don't know what it means to serve their country. See how many of them could walk around with a musket ball in their hip. Bunch of sissies with manicures."

"A woman after my own heart," someone said from the shadows. His voice was deep and smooth as whiskey. "That's why Ugly Mo bypasses the government at all costs."

When he came out of the shadows it took everything I had not to flinch. Scarlet wasn't so subtle.

"Good Lord, you're *ugly*," she said. "I've never seen somebody so ugly. Would you look at that, Addison? Are you ugly natural, or did you have some kind of accident?" she asked him. "That's how superheroes are born, you know. Maybe you fell into a meat grinder or some radiation."

I grabbed Scarlet and pulled her close, clamping my hand over her mouth. About twenty years ago Scarlet had reached the age where she'd decided she could say whatever she wanted to and ignore all social niceties. She called it an old lady pass. I was pretty sure she was the only one who enjoyed that particular freedom.

"I apologize for my Aunt Scarlet. She has an old lady pass, so she thinks she doesn't have to be polite anymore."

Ugly Mo stared at us out of dead black eyes. He was blacker than coal and bald as a billiard, his face horribly disfigured. One of his eyes bugged out and never seemed to focus on anything. His face was scarred and part of his nose was missing. He wore a three-piece suit the color of limes and a bright red tie. And he walked with a cane, though I was willing to bet money it wasn't *just* a cane.

Scarlet bit the inside of my hand and I jerked it away, rubbing it on my leggings. Mo kept staring at Scarlet for several seconds, but she didn't bat an eyelash. And then he dropped his head back and laughed. A big booming sound that echoed in the cavernous space.

"I've always been ugly," he said, wiping tears from his eyes. "House fire when I was seventeen didn't help matters any. Never kept me from catching the pussy though. Know what I'm saying?"

"I hear ya," Scarlet said, nodding and putting away her gun. "It's all in the technique. Young people these days don't understand the mechanics."

Ugly Mo and Scarlet did a knuckle bump, and I was starting to wonder if I was in an episode of *The Twilight Zone*.

"Whew, lady," Mo said, looking Scarlet's face

over. "You been in a tussle. You need Mo to put a cap in somebody's ass for mistreating a lady?"

"Already taken care of," Scarlet said. "Shot his ear right off."

"You're one tough bitch. They don't make bitches like you no more."

"Oh, go on with yourself," Scarlet said, blushing like a schoolgirl.

"You must be Addison Holmes," Mo said, turning to me. "Jimmy Royal said you're in need of my van," Mo said. "It's right back here. Just finished up the detailing on it yesterday."

I looked around at the junkyard of cars, not seeing anything that remotely resembled a van and said, "Umm." I was going to kill Jimmy Royal.

"I got just what you need." Mo stamped his cane against the cement for emphasis. "You'll be the most badass P.I. in Savannah. It's a genuine Mercedes Benz motorhome, barely used. It's got a fresh coat of paint and a couple upgrades on the interior. And due to the fact that I need room for more inventory on the floor, I'm going to cut you a special deal."

He headed toward the back of the warehouse and Scarlet and I followed, passing old junkers mingled with a couple of brand new Honda Accords that I was almost positive weren't there by legal means. There was still a car seat in the back of one of them.

Mo flicked on another set of lights, illuminating the back half of the warehouse, and I almost choked on my tongue. It looked like a new car showroom, everything polished to a shine.

"Holy crap," Scarlet said. "This here's the kind of car I always thought would complement my personality."

I looked at the bright yellow Ferrari with raised eyebrows. I'd always kind of seen Scarlet in a tank.

"That's a mighty fine car there, Miss Scarlet. It would suit you real nice. But that one's already sold. Most of these cars are being shipped out tonight. We do a real fast turnaround here at Ugly Mo's."

"I see that," Scarlet said thoughtfully. "Maybe I need to think about investing in the car business."

"Big Mo would be happy to have you as an investor."

"Is that the van?" I asked, pointing to the black Mercedes that was parked just inside the garage doors that led to the back side of the lot.

"That's not a van," Mo corrected. "That's an *experience*. It has all the comforts of home on four tires."

Considering I didn't have a home at the moment, it was sounding better and better by the second. The rain was really coming down now, droplets pelting against the tin roof like a hail of bullets. I could feel the electrical currents building. The hair on my arms was standing straight up.

"Have you ever thought about having short hair?" Mo said. "Seems like a lot less maintenance. My old lady got short hair and that way she can wear whatever wig she wants to on top. Seems like a lot more opportunity for variety."

"I'm going to take her to the salon after we're done here," Scarlet piped in before I could answer. "My stylist is a real genius. Addison's got hair just like mine when I was younger. If you don't maintain it and keep it in good condition it starts to take on a mind of its own." Then she switched topics. "You can do some damn fine investigating in that little thing. We'll be a force to be reckoned with. And it's black, so no one will ever suspect us of spying on them."

"*We?*" I asked.

But Scarlet ignored me. "How much does a fine piece of machinery like this cost?"

Ugly Mo rattled off a number that would have made my testicles run and hide for cover if I'd had any.

I sputtered before asking, "Jimmy Royal was able to afford something like that?"

"Oh, no. Jimmy Royal got the economy edition. He's got all that child support to pay. This is the top of the line."

"Well, I can't afford that. Do you have another economy edition?"

"Nope, this is it, but maybe we can work out a trade," Ugly Mo said.

"That's how business was done back in the day," Scarlet said. "The barter system. When I worked for the OSS I'd find my mark, seduce him into telling me everything he knew, and then take all his money before the authorities could come take him off to be tortured for more information."

"That's not that barter system at all, Aunt Scarlet," I said, horrified.

"Oh. Then I don't know what I'm talking about. I'll let the two of you work out the details."

"What if I knock it down to half-price?" he asked. "Would that be more doable?"

"Sure," I said. "I could do that. What's the catch?"

"I've got a little bit of an issue with my old lady. I've been suspicious of her activities lately. Seems my competitor has known of a few of my dealings and intercepted a shipment or two, and Jasmine has been acting real secretive. And she's been overdoing it on the sex too. We been together thirteen years. I ain't never had so many blowjobs in my life, and you know that's not something a woman just volunteers unless something's going on. I figure a private investigator could clear things up real quick."

I bit my lip. I really wanted that van. It would cover my immediate housing and transportation needs. But there was one problem. "It's against agency policy to take side jobs," I told Mo. "Everything has to go through the agency."

"Oh, bollocks to that," Scarlet said. "I'll take the job. And then you can help me with it and you don't have to worry about all those dumb rules." She turned to Mo. "Never in my life have I met someone so caught up with the rules. Her sister's not like that at all. Would talk you out of your life savings without batting an eyelash. And she's got some of that medicinal marijuana too."

"Love that stuff," Mo said. "Helps my arthritis. Used to be a clinic right here in town, but the cops swooped in and shut it down. If I ever find the bastard responsible for taking away such a service to the community I'm going to hunt him down like a dog."

Heat flushed through my entire body and I had that clammy feeling you get just before you're about to throw up everywhere. I knew the clinic Mo was talking about. I'd busted a senior citizen who'd been growing at the assisted living facility he lived at, and then selling to the clinic in town. So I guess I was the one responsible for shutting down Savannah's largest-growing pot industry.

"What's this Jasmine look like?" Scarlet asked. "You got the deets on her?"

I raised my brows at the slang, while I ignored the impending feeling of doom. We needed to leave. I was getting antsy.

"Her picture is painted on the front of the building, but I can probably send you more details through email. You do this favor for me and you'll always be in Ugly Mo's favor."

"You've got a deal," Scarlet said, knuckle bumping him again.

I wasn't really sure what had just happened or how things had spiraled out of control so quickly. I'd just wanted a van. And now I was getting a van with a whole lot of strings attached and I'd somehow become fifty-fifty partners with Scarlet in a business I hadn't known we'd started.

"How about real license plates and a new VIN number?" I asked. "Am I going to have any trouble with the police?"

"It's a hundred percent police proof," Mo said. "But maybe be careful driving it in the Forsyth Park area. Just in case."

Before I knew what was happening I'd passed over the biggest check I'd ever written, and I was holding the keys. Ugly Mo handed me a title and some other paperwork, and Scarlet and I piled into my new vehicle and we drove out of the building and into the pouring rain. The seats were leather and heated, and if anyone wanted this puppy back they were going to have to pry the keys out of my cold, dead hands.

"He seemed like a nice man," Scarlet said. "I've

always appreciated entrepreneurs like Ugly Mo. They're real go-getters."

"He's a car thief," I said.

"Everyone's got to start somewhere. And look at all the good that's come out of meeting him. You've got a brand new car at half-off and we get to turn in that lying, cheating Jasmine, and keep Mo from losing more business."

"Innocent until proven guilty."

"I don't know what rock you just crawled out from under, but that's not the way the system works. All you got to do is call Jasmine out on Twitter and she's as good as guilty."

I took Martin Luther King Street all the way to Bay to avoid the smaller street traffic. The sidewalks were clear of pedestrians because of the weather, but street traffic was a nightmare. Horns were blaring and I'd gotten a few rude gestures. I didn't realize until we were halfway down the street that people were just returning the favor, since Scarlet had been giving the one-finger salute the whole time.

"Stop doing that," I said. "It's rude."

"I know, but I can't seem to help myself. I think there's a switch in the brain that flips when you hit eighty. Most of the people I know died long before then, so it's kind of like a rite of passage. There's so many damn rules to live by in polite society. When you're standing in a long line at the post office don't you ever have the urge to start ripping packages out of people's hands and telling the only cashier at the register to go fuck himself?"

Actually, I'd had those exact feelings the last time I'd been at the post office. But I still had the before-eighty polite switch that told me I shouldn't do it.

"You didn't actually do that did you?" I asked.

"No, but that's only because everyone in front of me let me cut in line because I'm an old lady and I might have faked being unable to stand that long."

"Good thinking."

I was headed back to the agency when Scarlet pointed and said, "Grab that parking spot. It's like the stars are aligning for me today. I need to buy a lottery ticket."

"Your face is swollen and you've got two black eyes. How is today going in your favor?"

"You heard Mo. I'm one tough bitch. And

when a parking spot opens up in front of one of the most exclusive salons in Savannah, you don't kick the universe in the balls as a thank you."

I slammed on the brakes and both of us jerked against the seatbelt. I hadn't prepared myself to actually visit Scarlet's salon. I hadn't been serious about a change. Well, maybe I'd been serious, but I had to think about it a little more. What kind of drastic changes did I want to make? Julia Roberts in *Steel Magnolias* drastic or Charlize Theron in *Mad Max* drastic? Actually, probably neither were good choices for me.

A horn blared behind me and I waved in apology before trying to figure out the best way to sidewalk park in downtown Savannah. There was no way I could parallel park. I couldn't parallel park the smallest of cars. So I just pulled in front forward and left the back end sticking out into the street a little.

"We don't have to do this today," I said, pure panic taking over my body. I'd rather deal with a dead body any day. "She's probably booked. And you're probably still not feeling too good."

"I'm fit as a fiddle," Scarlet said, hopping out of the van.

I thunked my head against the steering wheel once and then got out to join Scarlet on the sidewalk. It's not like my hair could get much worse. The rain was pelting right off of Scarlet's hair like she was wearing a helmet. I had rivulets of water running down my scalp and into my eyes. I probably looked like a drowned rat.

My theory was confirmed when we walked in the salon and the receptionist squeaked at the sight of me.

"My niece here needs to see Chermaine," Scarlet said. "This is an emergency, and I won't take no for an answer."

The poor girl looked terrified of Scarlet and she ran to the back to warn Chermaine of our arrival. I wasn't really sure what to do other than drip on the carpet.

Before I knew what was happening I was being ushered to the back and a girl was pulling my sweater over my head and wrapping me in a black robe. A glass of champagne was shoved in my hand, I was led to a chair that looked vaguely similar to the one in my gynecologist's office, and hot compresses were applied to my neck, abdomen, and feet. I was told I looked tense. That was an understatement.

I downed the champagne in one gulp and the girl refilled it. I was guessing she was Chermaine's assistant, though she looked terrified and ready to jump out of her skin. And then a woman walked in, and I could understand why the assistant looked like she was on her last pair of Depends.

"I am Chermaine," the woman announced in a thickly Slavic accent. She posed in the doorway so I could take it all in, and I took another healthy sip of champagne.

She was an Amazon, well over six feet and thickly boned. Her head was shaved except for the strip of fuchsia hair that ran down the center of her head gelled into dangerous looking spikes at least a foot long. She wore a skintight black cat suit, but she'd embellished it with a bandolier across her chest and a thigh holster. Instead of bullets in the bandolier she had various pieces of hairdressing equipment—combs, brushes, hair clips, and a straight razor. In the thigh holder was a pair of wickedly sharp scissors.

"You are Scarlet's niece?" she asked, arching a black brow at me.

I only nodded because I was incapable of

speech.

"Scarlet is one of my favorites. She reminds me much of Chermaine. I've seen pictures of Scarlet's youth and can see the resemblance. You have good bones. Good genes," she said, coming slowly into the room, looking me up and down like a prized horse. "Terrible hair," she continued. "But Chermaine will fix."

"I…I just want a trim," I said.

"Silence," she barked. "You do not tell Picasso what to paint. Just as you do not tell Chermaine how to cut. Chermaine can see into the soul and envision the cut you need. You are looking for change. For adventure. But you are not brave enough to be adventurous with color. We will go short. Very short. Like a pixie. Your cheekbones and eyes will pop. You will be magnificent, as much as your prurient soul will allow. This hair will get you much sex. The men will love it."

"I'm sort of on a sex break," I said.

"Nonsense," she said, clapping her hands and jerking the assistant to attention. "You will be naked before the morrow. Chermaine knows and sees all. Esmerelda, take her to be washed. We have much work to do in very little time."

I LOST TRACK of time. I only remember looking up at one point and seeing Scarlet laid out next to me in an identical magical chair, her face covered in some kind of blue goop with green gel patches over her eyes. I think they waxed my eyebrows at some point, but the champagne had made me sleepy, so I might have dozed off. I could have stayed in Chermaine's care for the rest of my life. I might look like a horror story by the time she was finished, but I *felt* amazing.

They pulled the eye pads and all of the heated wraps off, and then the chair contorted to an upright position. Scarlet was standing in front of me, the bruising on her face much reduced.

"Holy cow," we both said at the same time.

"The swelling on your face is almost gone," I said in amazement.

"Holy cow," she said again, staring at my hair. "You look just like Anne Hathaway. But not all prostitute-like and emaciated like she was in Les Mis."

"Chermaine does not make mistakes," Chermaine said, turning the chair so I faced the mirror.

I didn't recognize my reflection. And then I

did and I burst into tears. Not because the haircut was bad, but because it was a heck of a shock. I had Audrey Hepburn hair. I looked like a complete stranger.

"Cease," Chermaine said. "Chermaine doesn't allow tears in her presence. You are weak. Beautiful, but weak. Now get out of my chair and go prepare for your sex."

Scarlet took my credit card and paid for me since I seemed incapable of doing anything else. And then we bundled up and went back into the rain to the van. When I looked in the rearview mirror, my hair was in exactly the same spot as it had been inside the salon. And there was no frizz or hair expansion. It was a miracle.

I was on auto-pilot, so I headed toward the Dairy Queen out of habit. There were no words spoken other than what we used to place our orders. I got my typical hot fudge with extra fudge and nuts and Scarlet got strawberry.

"You can just drop me at the hotel," Scarlet said. "I'm an old lady and I need my rest. I want to look my best for church in the morning. Ugly Mo sent me a text and invited me to come to his church. I always wanted to go to a black church.

They got better music than the Methodist church. And they always wear pretty hats. I got a red hat I've been saving for a special occasion."

"Sounds like fun," I said, pulling up in front of the historic inn Scarlet made her home while in Savannah. I helped her out of the front seat, handing her over to the care of the bellman who knew her by name.

"Call me after church," Scarlet said. "We can get started on that case for Ugly Mo and that no-good Jasmine."

"Right," I said, wincing. I was going to have a lot of explaining to do to Kate.

CHAPTER SIX

Sunday (Barely)

I WOKE WITH a startled gasp as someone pounded on the van door.

By the time I'd dropped Scarlet off and headed back to the agency, I was plain tuckered out. I also wasn't ready to show anyone my haircut yet, so I avoided going inside the agency and skipped out on dinner with my mother and Vince.

I did call Kate and let her know what had happened between Scarlet and Ugly Mo so I could get a discount on my van. Kate said I could have the case with her blessing if I'd keep Scarlet out of the agency while she was in town. I figured that was probably a pretty good trade off.

Mo had sent me a file on Jasmine, including an actual photograph instead of the graffiti likeness, as well as her daily habits and friends. According to Mo, Saturday night was girl's night, because the weekends were big business for Mo and he wanted her out of the way while he was doing business. Jasmine and a group of her friends had VIP access at the Tiger Lounge from eight in the evening to two in the morning. The Tiger Lounge was a strip club on the outskirts of Savannah, and never in a million years would I fit in if I tried to go inside and get the scoop. The best I could hope was to catch her coming out when they were finished.

I wasn't about to call Scarlet for a midnight stakeout that might result in a whole lot of nothing, so I'd gone to bed early and set my alarm for twelve-thirty so I could get a feel for Jasmine Jackson. I'd chalk it up to basic recon and fill Scarlet in later.

I'd found a primo parking spot on the street in front of the agency, and technically, I was pretty sure I wasn't supposed to be sleeping in my van. But I figured no one would really know I was inside unless I kept the lights turned on or the generator running. Which pretty much made my camping experience miserable as I was cocooned under a mountain of blankets and I'd eaten my takeout Chinese in the dark.

The knocks sounded again. *Bang, bang, bang* in rapid succession. Someone knew I was inside, despite my attempts to go unnoticed. Or maybe they didn't know I was inside, but wanted to steal my very swanky new pad and they were checking first before they broke the window and hotwired the car. Maybe it was Ugly Mo's competitor.

I stayed stock still and picked up my phone to check the time, hiding it under the covers so no one saw the light. It was just past midnight. It wouldn't be long before my alarm went off. Whoever was at the door had cheated me out of twenty-two minutes of sleep.

"Addison, open the door," I heard Nick say. "It's an emergency."

I scrambled out of bed, stubbing my toe against the little table that I couldn't figure out how to fold back up into the wall. And then I hit my head on the cabinet above the sink.

"Ouch, dammit," I said, rubbing my head and hopping on one foot.

A thousand thoughts were going through my mind. I'd grown up the daughter of a cop and there was still that entrenched fear of another cop knocking on the door in the middle of the night to deliver bad news.

I fumbled for the door handle, still not familiar with the locks and mechanisms that worked the van, and I shoved the door open, whacking Nick right in the shoulder. A cold blast of wet ice blew in and smacked me right in the face.

"Ouch," Nick hissed, rubbing his shoulder and pushing me back as he came inside. He shut the door behind him and we stood in the dark in the tiny space.

"What happened?" I asked. "Who's dead? What's the emergency?"

"The emergency is it's fucking cold outside and it's sleeting. How are you staying warm in here? I thought I'd find you frozen like a popsicle."

"I've been buried under blankets trying to sleep. And now I'm cold because you woke me up." And then I thought about it. "Wait, how'd you know I was even in here? I just bought this thing today."

"Don't remind me. Ugly Mo isn't exactly known for his legitimate business practices."

"Are you having me followed?" I asked suspiciously, thinking he might be getting back at me for putting the tracker on his car. And then I realized my phone hadn't vibrated to alert me Nick was in the area.

As if he were reading my mind he smiled and said, "I took the Audi. You forgot to put a tracker on that one. And of course I'm not having you followed. I'm a cop. You're not exactly known for your subtle behavior. I get phone calls at all hours reciting your misfortunes. By the time I got to the scene this morning I knew what kind of donuts were in the box. I don't have men watching you, but there are plenty of cops whose job it is to watch Ugly Mo."

"I feel like my rights are being violated."

"Try being a cop," he said wryly. "You'll get used to it." He turned on the flashlight on his phone and the area lit up.

"I thought you looked different," he said, staring at my hair. "What happened to your hair?"

I narrowed my eyes. "What do you mean, what happened to my hair? I got a haircut. And I like it."

"Hey, I like it too. It just took me off guard. You look like Anne Hathaway. But not when she was a toothless prostitute. After she started gaining weight back after the movie."

"That's better," I said, nodding.

"It smells like Chinese in here. It's making me hungry. I just got off work."

"Any news on the Chandler murder/suicide?"

"Nope. We've been told in no uncertain terms to wrap up the investigation. That we're trying to find something that's not there because he was a cop."

"What do you think?" I asked.

I could tell Nick was pissed. Nick didn't often get pissed. He was pretty even-tempered, especially in tense situations, which was probably a good personality trait for someone who carried a gun and had to deal with people who were more than likely lying on a pretty regular basis.

"I think I don't really have a choice but to close it up and write the report. The mayor was very specific."

"I ate all the Chinese," I said apologetically.

"It's okay. I didn't come here to eat dinner. I really like your hair," he said again, touching the nape of my neck.

He took a step closer. Things were getting very warm, very quickly. I wasn't built to be in enclosed spaces with Nick for long periods of time. He had a pheromone problem. Or maybe it was me with the problem.

"Umm…you said something about an emergency," I said, swallowing heavily.

"Yep, it's a dire emergency. Life or death."

And then he kissed me and pulled me against him, and I realized it was a dire situation indeed. I wasn't sure how he'd gotten his pants zipped, but they practically popped right open when my hand brushed against the button.

Nick was one of those men who exuded sex. His body was a work of art and his face looked as if it had been sculpted by the gods. Thank goodness he'd broken his nose somewhere along the way, or he would've been too perfect to look at. This was the first relationship I'd ever been in where I hadn't had to come up with excuses to avoid sex. I'd always had the impression that maybe I just wasn't a sexual person. It turns out having sex with the right person made a big difference. Looking at him always turned me on, and I wondered how long it would last. I was hoping forever.

He jerked my sweatshirt over my head and I hitched my legs up so they wrapped around his waist. We wobbled unsteadily for a moment as he caught his balance and moved toward the back of the van.

"I thought I had another week," I said, panting. His mouth slid down my neck and I felt his fingers working at the ties of my pajama pants. My eyes crossed and I think I whimpered.

"You do, but if I wait another week I'm going to spontaneously combust."

"I've been spontaneously combusting for the last three weeks. Maybe you should've tried it to keep the edge off."

"Are you complaining?" he asked, nipping my bottom lip. His hand slipped beneath my elastic waistband and felt firsthand that I wasn't complaining at all.

"Nope, not me," I said.

There was a lot of cursing and bumping into things on the way to the little bed I'd been sleeping in. I was pretty sure we weren't going to fit, but Nick was very creative when it came to sex. And truth be told, spontaneously combusting on my own wasn't doing it for me anymore.

There were times for romance and finesse. This wasn't one of those times. A few minutes later we were both sweaty and naked, trying to catch our breaths.

"I've made my decision," I said, sprawled half-way on top of Nick. "I'll marry you."

"Nope, you've still got a week to decide. I'd don't want you to say later on that you were coerced."

I blew out a breath and knew he was right. I wasn't capable of making rational decisions at the moment. A man who knew his elbow from a G-spot was a hot commodity. Then I heard my mother's voice in my head saying, "Act in haste, repent at leisure," and I shuddered, wondering why I was thinking of my mother.

"What's wrong?" Nick asked.

"I might have pulled a muscle," I said, just to change the subject.

"That explains the weird sounds. I didn't re-member you being such a screamer."

His heart pounded against my ear. "You think people could hear us?"

"On the off-chance that a group of people were gathered around the van in the sleet and cold, then yes, they could probably hear us. Besides, you know we rocked this thing. Anyone driving down the street probably knew what was going on."

"Ohmigosh," I said, embarrassment flushing my body. "My mother is going to find out."

"Your fear of your mother finding out things is a little weird. You're a grown woman. What's she going to do to you?"

"It's just the principle of the thing. She'll give me that mom look. It's terrifying."

"I'm guessing the mom look yours gave you growing up was much different than my mother's. I think the look isn't as effective when hazed with gin."

I looked up so I could see his face. Nick hadn't had the best childhood. Growing up with money hadn't meant a lot when affection from his parents had been tied to what he'd achieved. Nick becoming a cop had been his way of rebelling against them. He'd never expected to fall in love with the job. And they'd never forgiven him for it.

Light from the streetlamps seeped through the cracks of the blinds on the windows, and the stark angles of his face were cast in shadow. I shivered at the sight of him and he rubbed his hand up and down my arm soothingly. I sighed and snuggled closer.

"If it makes you feel better, your mom and

Vince got caught by a patrolman last week over in Thunderbolt."

"Got caught?" I asked.

"I think they've both lost their minds. Imagine getting caught bare-ass naked in the back of a car that's recognizable all over the state."

"Ohmigosh, why did you tell me that? They got caught having *sex*?"

"What did you think I meant? It wouldn't have been near as exciting if they'd got caught playing checkers. Vince flashed his badge, so it was no big deal, but you know how the gossip spreads."

"They're like teenagers ever since they got married. Can't even sleep in the house with them they're so loud. They're old enough to know better."

"Your mom is only in her fifties. I think Vince is too. Fifty is the new thirty. You and me, babe, we're going to still be rocking the van a couple of decades from now."

The alarm on my phone went off, and we both jumped at the intrusion. I'd completely forgotten that I'd set it.

"Oh, crap," I muttered, fumbling across the

tiny bed for the phone I'd left on the table. "I've got to work. And I need to shower. I smell like sex."

"You're working tonight?" Nick asked incredulously. "You can't go out in this weather. No one knows how to drive in this stuff. This is the south. People lose their damn minds when anything frozen falls from the sky."

"Ugly Mo hired me to find out if his old lady is selling her body and his secrets to his competitor."

I felt Nick go stiff, and not in the way I'd just enjoyed. "I'm assuming you turned him down, since it's against Kate's policy to take outside jobs."

"Nope, I didn't really have a choice. Aunt Scarlet accepted on my behalf."

"That's a mess you don't want to get in the middle of." Nick sat up and started pulling on his clothes. "Ugly Mo is a criminal, but he's mostly a criminal with a conscience. Fat Louie is a cold-blooded killer. If Mo's old lady is two-timing him with Louie, then she's as good as dead. Mo would kick her out. But Louie will keep her until she's outlasted her usefulness, and then we'll find her body in the river with her throat slit."

"I've just got to follow her around a couple of days and give a report to Mo. We made a trade for the van. I can't go back on my word. Besides, Kate gave me permission."

He stood and was practically vibrating with anger. "How is it that you keep finding yourself in situations like this? Everyone in this city knows to stay out of Ugly Mo and Fat Louie's business. The cops have been watching them for years with nothing to show for it except two dead undercover agents who got too close to Fat Louie. How are you going to keep yourself alive if you don't bother to learn what the dangers are? Naivety isn't an excuse anymore. If this is your job, then you need to know the score and learn the best ways to stay alive. I'm not marrying you so I can become a widower."

I haphazardly pulled on my clothes, my own temper in full steam now. "You won't have to worry about that because I'm not marrying you."

"Yes, you are. You just said so."

"I take it back," I yelled. "And stop telling me how to do my job. Kate didn't seem overly concerned about it. I'm not an idiot. I'm armed and I can take care of myself. Last time I checked I'm a better shot than you are."

That was hitting below the belt and still a sore subject for Nick. He hadn't expected me to be an expert marksman. I'd grown up with a gun in my hand. That had been me and my dad's bonding time.

"Be that as it may," Nick said coldly, the frigidness of his words making me shiver. "You're still a woman about to go out in the middle of the night in what I'm assuming is going to be a bad part of town. You'd better hope Ugly Mo put in bulletproof glass. Sitting on the side of the road in a vehicle like this is asking for trouble. And if Fat Louie finds out what you're up to, moving out of state is your best bet. But still not enough. He'll find you."

"If you'll excuse me, I need to get to work," I said, just as coldly. I did it better than he did. He might have been born from an ice queen, but I was a Southern woman with an attitude. We invented frigidity.

Nick muttered something under his breath and I was pretty sure I could pick out the words *stubborn* and *foolish*. He zipped up his jacket and pulled a watch cap out of his pocket, slipping it on his head.

"I'll check in later," he said, opening the door and letting in a rush of cold air and icy rain. "I'm off this weekend."

"Fine," I said, feeling slightly let down that there were no slammed doors.

I turned on all the lights and cranked the generator. I had just over an hour to get to the other side of town and see what Jasmine Jackson was up to. My clothes were on inside out and I was only wearing one sock. I needed a strong pot of coffee and a hot shower.

CHAPTER SEVEN

I ENDED UP getting the shower and the coffee from inside the agency. I wasn't ready to rough it in the van yet, especially considering I hadn't stocked it with fluffy towels or body wash. Or toilet paper. Though that was easily remedied after I "borrowed" some from the employee bathroom.

I wasn't completely sure why I was mad at Nick. Probably because he was mad at me, and that was my typical reaction when someone got upset with me. I wasn't very good at taking criticism. At least not at first. Once I had time to let things soak in, I usually found that the person giving the criticism was at least partially right, but I came from a long line of stubborn women. Besides, Nick knew me well enough to know that's how I'd react. It seemed to me he'd try a different approach if he didn't want me to fly off the handle.

I knew he was worried, but this was my job, and it wasn't going to change. We'd had the same argument before, and it usually ended in the same way. The last time he hadn't been happy about my job he'd broken up with me after I'd been shot, though I could totally see his point. Bullets added a whole new level of realism to a relationship.

I don't think he'd actually broken up with me this time, but it seemed like boggy ground. And to his credit, I could see why he might be worried. I was a magnet for disaster. But I usually learned from my experiences, and other than the sunburn I got at the nudist colony, it had been a while since I'd been injured on the job.

Nick was right about one thing though. No one knew how the hell to drive when ice started falling from the sky. It took me half an hour to get to the highway, and I passed several fender benders along the way. Everyone else was going at a snail's pace, and an enterprising young man on the corner was selling cat litter. I still wasn't sure what that was for. Were we supposed to scatter it in the streets? Keep it in the trunk? Hit someone over the head with it and take their coat? It was a toss-up, but the guy on the corner was making a killing.

By the time I made it to the Tiger Lounge it was about ten minutes until two. I circled the block a couple of times, amazed that many people had decided a strip club selling lots of alcohol was a good idea on a night the roads were going to freeze over, but what did I know?

The Tiger Lounge was housed in an old, two-story wooden building that looked to be violating several city codes, at least from outside appearances. The roof had once been red, but had faded over time, and a balcony went around the entire second floor. I could see the ice building up on the railing, and bit my lip in indecision. It was dumb to be out in weather like this. And when this place shut down and everyone started getting in their cars it was going to be really dumb to be out. Georgia did not deal well with weather that included anything but dry.

Lights flashed between the cracks of rickety boards, and I could feel the vibration of the bass beneath my tires. No one was standing outside, but I had the feeling there were eyes everywhere.

The street was lined with cars on both sides, and even the neighboring streets were full. I saw a car leave about a hundred yards from the building and slipped into the spot, thankful that it was at the end of the block so I didn't have to parallel park between two cars. I turned off my lights and double-checked that all the doors were locked. It really wasn't a good neighborhood. And then I pulled out my binoculars.

I hadn't been sitting there for five minutes before I watched someone bust a window on the Lexus a few cars up and snatch something out of the front seat. I took my weapon out from under the seat and set it on my lap. Just in case anyone got any ideas.

A black Escalade passed by me and I watched with interest as it slowed to a stop in front of the Tiger Lounge doors. The license plate said UG-MO3, so I was thinking chances were pretty good that the car belonged to Ugly Mo. The front door of the club opened and a gaggle of cackling women hustled out, wearing less clothes than they should've been on a night like this. They didn't seem to notice the cold.

I recognized Jasmine immediately, even though her hair was different than her picture. I remembered Mo saying she wore wigs to change things up a little, and tonight she'd chosen a platinum blonde number that barely reached her chin. The picture of her spray-painted on the side of the building hadn't done her breasts justice. They were enormous and barely contained in a poison-green Lycra dress that stopped just short of showing everyone her preferred method of bikini maintenance.

The doors to the Escalade opened and just as the women started to get in, something hit against the side of the van, rocking it back and forth. My heart stopped and fear gripped its icy fingers around my spine. And then I heard the maniacal cackle of someone not altogether sane, and chills pebbled across my skin.

"Little bitch, little bitch, let me in," he called out in a sing-song voice. And then his face appeared in my window, and a strange sound escaped my throat.

I shook my head no, sure that he saw the fear in my eyes. My hand gripped the gun comfortably and I thought just once I should probably start taking Nick's advice when he tried giving me orders. He only had my best interests at heart, after all.

My would-be attacker smiled, his face bony,

the flesh stretched across his skull grotesquely. He was mixed race, but looked mostly Hispanic, and he had tattoos across his face and neck. There was a smudged image on his right cheek I couldn't really make out, but the words "Property of FL" were stamped on his other cheek.

My first thought was that job interviews were probably a real challenge for him. My second thought was that I was staring into the face of a cold-blooded killer. He had piercings through almost every part of his face and ears, and one of his incisors was gold. He was wearing a black hoodie and kept tapping his crowbar against my window.

I was pretty sure I was going to die, and it would be horrible. But I was a cop's daughter, and if I was going to die, I'd make sure I went down in a blaze of glory. I held the gun up, leveling it at him.

He stared down the barrel of the gun for a few seconds and then laughed, that same maniacal laughter that crawled across my skin. My fear quotient went up ten-fold. There wasn't a lot you could do to fight crazy.

I knew I'd missed my window with Jasmine.

They were probably long gone by now, and if she was riding home in one of Ugly Mo's personal vehicles, chances were she wasn't making stops along the way to meet with his archenemy.

That left me and my killer in a standoff. There was no way I was letting go of the gun. And I couldn't reach across to put the car in gear with my left hand. It was time to piss or get off the pot, as my grandfather used to say.

I hit the button on the door and the window rolled down. Icy rain slapped across my face, but I didn't flinch. Flinching meant death.

"I will shoot you without regret," I said evenly. Sometimes I amazed myself at my bravado. I was almost positive I was going to have to change my pants when I got back.

"I like feisty bitches," he said. "Especially ones that look like that movie star."

"Anne Hathaway?" I asked.

"Nah, Audrey Hepburn. I like the classics."

"I can see that now," I said, gesturing toward his face with the gun. "I couldn't make out the Betty Boop on the side of your cheek before."

"Betty Boop is primo pussy."

"Nothing can get a guy off like a cartoon," I

said. "Look how popular Jessica Rabbit is."

"Smart-mouthed bitch," he said. "I got something that'll fill that mouth up. Big Eddie's going to have fun with you tonight. I bet you got primo pussy too."

"I take it you're Big Eddie?" I asked with a lot more courage than I was feeling.

"In the flesh. Want to see?" He grabbed his crotch and cackled again.

"I'll pass. You should probably stick with Betty Boop. My pussy is used to real men." He made a move forward and my finger squeezed just slightly on the trigger, enough that I could hear that first warning click. It was slight sound, more of a feel than anything. If I kept squeezing, a bullet was going to go into his head.

"I'm going to fuck you up, bitch."

"Maybe, but it's not going to be tonight. I come from a long line of crazy women. My grandma drove her car straight through a Western Sizzler just because she couldn't get to the dry cleaners on the other side. Last year, I ran over my ex-fiancé. And yesterday, my aunt shot the ear off some asshole who tried to rob a gas station."

"Get the fuck out," he said incredulously, taking a step back. "Your auntie shot Javier's ear off?"

"And she liked it," I said for good measure.

"That's cold. I heard they couldn't reattach it."

I moved the gun slightly to the left, so it was pointed toward his ear. "Maybe that's what I'll do. I think death is too easy for someone like you."

Big Eddie narrowed his eyes at me and we stared each other down for a few minutes. And then he said something about crazy bitches and backed off into the shadows.

Thank God I'd left the van running. I put it in gear and got the hell out of there. I ran through a couple of stop signs and was shaking by the time I made it back to the highway. The roads had started to freeze and the tires were finding the occasional patch of ice, adding to my panic. And it was the middle of the night and everything was closed except for the 24-hour Walgreens.

I parked in the fire zone and ran inside to grab an emergency pint of Haagan Dazs. Drastic times called for drastic measures, so I grabbed Rocky Road instead of plain chocolate. I was proud of myself because I managed to restrain myself from impulse-buying a value-pack of fun-size Snickers, the two-for-one boxed wine, and a thirty-six pack of condoms that were ribbed for my pleasure. They sure knew how to cater to the late night crowd.

It took me almost ten minutes to drive the three blocks to the agency. I was driving at a snail's pace due to the icy spots on the road, and the fact that I was trying to eat my ice cream one-handed. It was after three in the morning and no one else was out and about.

I parked in my same spot right in front of the agency and sat quiet for a few minutes to see if anyone was lurking in the area. The van felt too exposed. I didn't know if I'd ever be able to sleep in it comfortably without the fear of someone crashing into me or blowing holes through the side, a la Bonnie and Clyde. And maybe I shouldn't have bought a Mercedes. A Mercedes probably didn't blend in in the projects unless it belonged to a drug dealer. And more likely than not, recreational vehicles were probably not a drug dealer's first choice.

With my mind made up, I grabbed my clothes and headed back inside the agency where it might be slightly more difficult to kill me in my sleep. If I was going to die, I didn't want to know about it, so I took an over-the-counter sleeping pill, pushed a chair under the doorknob, and snuggled under the covers on the tiny mattress.

I WOKE THE next morning to my phone vibrating against my cheek. I must've rolled over on it sometime during the night.

" 'Lo," I answered.

I remembered why I hated taking sleeping pills. They made me feel like a slug for at least a couple of hours the next morning. I could barely lift my head up.

"Addison?" Rosemarie asked. "Is that you?"

" 'S'me," I slurred. " 'S'up?"

There was a pregnant pause before she started talking again. "I was just calling to check on you. You made a couple of weird phone calls to me last night. Are you okay?"

"Sleeping pill. Makes me drunk dial."

"Oh, that makes more sense. Couldn't make out what you were telling me. Something about Betty Boop and boxed wine. Thought Scarlet had taught you some of that Navaho code from during the war."

My mind, as foggy as it was, had its own mental breakdown at that sentence.

"Anyway," she went on. "I headed straight over after church. I'm circling the block now. I felt guilty not coming to check on you after your phone calls. I would've called Nick to come check on you, but I didn't have his private number, and I wasn't sure it was worthy of a call to 9-1-1. I spent the whole morning praying you weren't laying in a ditch somewhere."

"I'm fine. Got work. Missing organs." My mind felt like mush, but I was functional enough to know two things. One: Coffee would help if I drank a whole lot of it. Two: I didn't have the energy for Rosemarie.

"Organs?" she asked. "Who would steal an organ? They're so bulky and all the good ones are inside churches. What kind of person would steal the Lord's music? That doesn't even make sense. Maybe you need to see a doctor."

"Internal organs," I said. "Hearts, kidneys...that kind of thing."

"I read something about that on the travel channel once. They were talking about American tourists traveling to all these exotic countries and sometimes they'd just go missing. Organs are a delicacy in a lot of cultures, so these tribes would snatch these people up and cut out their organs like in Temple of Doom. Then they'd burn the bodies and grind the organ meat up for some kind of stew. Turns my stomach just to think about it."

"Mmm-hmm," I said, swallowing hard and dropping my head back to my pillow. I heard a horn blare and moved the phone away from my ear.

"Good grief, people," Rosemarie muttered. "They've salted all the streets. A bunch of idiots behind the wheel."

"It was bad last night," I said.

"Sun's out now, so it's melting, but the people in this city don't have the sense God gave a goose. I don't know how you can stand to live right in the thick of it. Don't you miss Whiskey Bayou?"

"Nope," I said. If I was sure of one thing in my life it was that I in no way, shape, or form missed living in Whiskey Bayou.

"That's odd. People are always asking about you."

"I'm sure they are. I kept the local gossip column in business the last couple of years. Bunch of busybodies."

"Which reminds me," Rosemarie said. "Your mother said to tell you hello, and that she hopes you'll find the time to visit the church that is literally next door to you some Sunday. Even I felt guilty after listening to her talk."

The detective agency was right next to the Trinity Methodist Church. It had been built in the mid-eighteen-hundreds, so it's not like I could give the excuse that I didn't know it was there.

"She's really good at the guilt part," I said.

"We almost didn't have church at all," Rosemarie went on excitedly. "It iced over real bad last night, and you know the city has both thumbs right up their ass when it comes to doing things like salting the streets. Walter Mosely tried parking in his usual handicap spot by the door, even though we all know that man's about as handicapped as Evander Holyfield with that little piece of his ear missing. Damn ridiculous if you ask me."

"Wha?" I asked, confused.

"Well, Walter pulled into his spot like usual, but it was slick as owl poop, and he just slid right on through. Took the handicapped sign with him and all those crepe myrtles. His car finally stopped just inches from the church wall. I told Pastor Frank that was probably the best thing that's happened in a long time. All the sinners came running out of their houses to see what had happened, and then they felt guilty once the excitement had died down, so they just moseyed over and finished out the church service. Biggest crowd I've seen since last Easter."

I put Rosemarie on speaker and let her talk, and then I rolled out of bed and crawled on my hands and knees for a bit to work out the kinks. The chair was still lodged under the door, and there was nothing but silence on the other side. It was rare for anyone to come into the office on Sundays. And Kate never came in.

I had a one-cup Keurig in my office and popped in a pod to take the edge off. I caught my reflection in the little silver part of the machine and let out a little squeak at the stranger that stared back at me. I'd forgotten about my hair.

"Addison, are you okay? I tell you, you're just not acting like yourself lately. I'm your friend, and I've got only your best interests at heart, but I think you need to marry that man already. It's ridiculous to keep yourself tied up in knots like this. It's not good for your digestion. And you get real cranky when you go too long without sex."

I hmmmed noncommittally, not willing to share that I'd had a minor lapse in judgment in my month-long sabbatical. And what had it solved? Not a damn thing. We'd scratched the itch and immediately started fighting. I could certainly understand why wars had been won and lost over sex. It was a powerful thing. Especially if Nick was doing the sexing.

Being friends with Rosemarie was always a unique experience. It really depended on what day of the week or what time of day it was. There was teacher Rosemarie, who wore flamingo-patterned capris and big, boxy denim shirts. There was nighttime party Rosemarie, who wore lots of pleather and enjoyed showing off her nipple rings. Then occasionally she'd bring out garage sale Rosemarie, slumber party Rosemarie, or tantric master Rosemarie, each of whom were identifiable by her wardrobe. But Sundays were saved for church lady Rosemarie. She had as many hobbies and clothing choices as Barbie. I had to admire her for it. She enjoyed every aspect of her life and lived it to the fullest.

"Oh, look," she said. "I found a parking spot. That's divine intervention right there. No one can ever find parking here on Sundays with the church services going. I think someone slipped out of services early. Bless their sinning soul."

I just stared at the trickle of black liquid filling my cup, willing it to go faster. I heard her car door slam and a couple of muffled mutters.

"Whew, this sidewalk is a hazard. Can you believe those bastards? They salted in front of the church but left the rest of the sidewalks icy. Not very Christian of them, if you ask me. Oh Lord, would you look at that?" Rosemarie said, hopping topics again. "Such crude language. I know I use my fair share of salty language, but never on the Lord's Day. And bastard is in the bible. And so is damn. So those doesn't count. I've got standards, unlike these heathens. And right on the Savannah streets in front of a church. I have a mind to find that van owner and give them a stern talking to. There are children that walk these roads."

"What?" I said, a horrible sinking feeling in the pit of my stomach.

"Somebody decided to use their van as a billboard. It looks ridiculous and I'll certainly never shop at their store, whatever it is. They didn't even put a website."

I scrambled around until I dug my UGGs out of the bag in the corner and shoved them on over my sweats. And then I hit my hip on the corner of the desk and banged my knees against the chair blocking the door. I jerked it out of the way and hauled ass down the hallway to the front doors.

I disarmed the alarm and opened the front door. And then it was lights out. I woke sometime later flat on the ground, wet seeping through my clothes, and Rosemarie staring down at me. Her golden halo of hair slightly flattened by the damp air.

"Are you okay?" she mouthed. I wondered why she wasn't speaking so I could hear her, and then the world whooshed back into full focus and I realized it was just me that couldn't hear.

"Is anything broken?" I asked, closing my eyes again. "I don't want to look. The second I look it'll start to hurt."

"It doesn't look like it," she said. "Nothing pointed in a weird direction. But Lordy, you scared the bejesus right out of me. The second your foot hit the top step you looked just like one of those cartoon characters stepping on a banana peel. You just went *wooft* and somersaulted right in the air. It was like slow motion, and then you rebounded off the pavement and went limp. Thought you were dead at first. And then the church bells started ringing and I figured that was a sign of your ascension. I didn't know whether to weep or start singing Nearer My God to Thee, so I did a little of both."

"Nothing hurts yet," I said.

"That's a bad sign. You've probably got one of those brain bleeds. Or maybe you're paralyzed from the neck down." She stared at me for a little bit, trying to puzzle something out, and then her face cleared as she figured it out.

"My, my, your hair is short. Just like a boy's. I knew something was different about you. If you hadn't gotten your hair cut you'd have had a little more padding and probably wouldn't have a brain bleed now."

"I don't have a brain bleed," I said, moving all my extremities, nice and slow. My head wasn't hurting, but my shoulder felt like it was on fire. I had a feeling it had taken the brunt of the fall.

Rosemarie hooked her arm in mine and helped

me to a sitting position. The world spun a little, but I closed my eyes and let everything settle. And then I opened my eyes. I wish I hadn't, because I got a good look at the van and a combination of anger and fear rioted through my body. Adrenaline was the best painkiller there was.

"Son of a bitch," I yelled out and then remembered where we were. I looked around to see if anyone had heard me, but the later church service hadn't let out yet.

"That's my new van," I said. At least they hadn't done any structural damage at first glance. But whoever it was had taken liberty with decorating the exterior. The words *CUNT BITCH* were spray-painted across the side.

"It says *DIE WHORE* on the other side and something in Spanish on the hood. I can only remember my colors and vegetables from the semester I took in college, so I wasn't able to translate."

I made a sound that was something between a wheeze and a scream. "That's my new van," I repeated.

"It's a real nice van," Rosemarie said, for lack of anything better. "And I've always been partial to that shade of orange. It really brightens things up on such a dreary day."

"Ugly Mo is going to be *pissed*," I thought aloud. "He just gave it a new paint job."

"You know," Rosemarie said. "I really feel like I missed a lot between now and when I dropped you off yesterday."

I sighed and felt my shoulders slump in defeat. After the excellent haircut I thought maybe things were starting to go my way. "It was a day for the books," I said. "I bought a van, got my hair cut, and did a stakeout over at the Tiger Lounge."

Rosemarie's cornflower-blue eyes widened. "The Tiger Lounge? On Claymore?"

"That's the one. I didn't really fit in."

"I can imagine. Can you stand?" she asked.

"Probably. I need to move the van before church lets out. My mother will surely hear about that. I think she has a direct line to God for certain infractions."

"I never really picture your mother as a real religious woman, even though she goes to church every Sunday like clockwork."

"I'd say she's more spiritual than religious," I said, hobbling to my feet. I walked it off, stretching my muscles to get the kinks out. "She's kind of like Oprah."

"That makes more sense. She's omnipotent."

"Basically. I've learned a lot about my mom since my dad died. Mostly that the first twenty-seven years of my life were a lie. I always wondered where Phoebe got her eccentric nature. It turns out it was from my mother. She just hid it during their marriage and pretended to be a genteel Southern lady who never missed a church service. She put on pantyhose and went to work at a job she hated, and she was always the PTA president and Girl Scout troop leader. When what she really wanted was to go to naked yoga three times a week and take pottery classes. I think that's why she's such a bad cook. Her subconscious was rebelling. Who cooks meals for thirty years and never gets better at it? Since my dad died I think she's been experimenting finding herself. I think she maybe still gets confused between the woman she used to be and the woman she's become."

"It's all about balance," Rosemarie said sagely. "I've got a friend over on Victory that owns a body shop. Maybe he can get this cleaned up for you."

"Okay, but I've really got to work. That check

from catching the Romeo Bandit isn't going to last long."

"You could always marry Nick," she said.

I put my hands on my hips, a little indignant. "I am not marrying Nick for his *money*."

"So does that mean you're marrying him for another reason?"

"Shut up," I said and narrowed my eyes.

Rosemarie just smiled, her point made. "You can follow me there, but you should probably change clothes and do something with your hair. You look like Liza Minelli. I'll move the van to a side street for you while you change, so the church people aren't traumatized."

I got the car keys and brought them back to Rosemarie, and then I headed for the bathroom. I took off my clothes and studied myself in the mirror before I got in the shower. I had a few scrapes here and there, and my shoulder was already purpling. All in all, it could've been a lot worse.

By the time I got out of the shower and the hot water had done its job, the left side of my body was a starburst of colors. My hip was also a nice, healthy eggplant shade. I dug around in the medicine cabinet and came up with some Icy Hot patches and a bottle of Tylenol. I stuck several patches to the worst areas and took twice the recommended dosage on the bottle of Tylenol.

I smelled somewhat reminiscent of my grandma Bertha when she lived in the nursing home—Mentholatum, Lever 2000 soap, and strained peas—only I lacked the strained peas smell.

I dressed quickly in new pair of leggings and a black tank top. I could already tell a bra would not be a comfortable addition, so I slapped a couple of Band-Aids over my nipples. Not the waterproof kind, because I'd made that mistake before.

I covered the tank top with a vintage Tears for Fears shirt that hung off one shoulder and also managed to cover my behind. I topped it all off with a black leather jacket, thinking the more layers I wore the more likely it was to cover the Icy Hot smell. Once I had on the leather jacket I decided to get out my ass-kicking boots.

Back when I was in the habit of living paycheck to paycheck and maxing out my credit cards, I'd bought a pair of black Saint Laurent rain boots that had silver studs from the ankles all the way to the knees. Since I'd never experienced the need to kick ass on the same day it was raining, I'd never actually worn the boots.

Actually, I wasn't much of an ass kicker on my most ass-kicking days—the previous night's behavior being the exception to the rule—but that was only because I was faced with a life or death situation. Mostly, I still expected people to use good manners and be polite when I asked them questions. Savannah was an interesting mix of old-school charm and modern assholery, so sometimes my expectations weren't met.

Between the boots, the jacket, and my Tears for Fears shirt, I was feeling pretty accomplished. And I could barely smell the Icy Hot anymore. I added a chain belt that hung low on my hips and bloused my shirt over it a little.

I put a little mousse in my hair to give it some texture and I slicked on some red lipstick. There were some days you had to make your own sunshine.

"Whoa," Rosemarie said as I came back down the front stairs twenty minutes later. "Are you working undercover in 1986?"

"I just felt like I needed to seize the day. I didn't start out on the best foot."

"That's good thinking. Now I wish I'd seized the day before I got dressed for church this morning. We don't match."

Rosemarie and I didn't look like we belonged on the same planet. We did, however, look like we belonged in the same decade, only I was wearing *The Breakfast Club* Collection and she was flirting the line somewhere between *Steel Magnolias* and *Heathers*.

She wore a turquoise wool dress that stopped mid-calf and made her legs look like logs that had been chopped in half. The dress had a row of double-breasted silver buttons that served absolutely no purpose whatsoever, and she was wearing black, patent leather heels and nude pantyhose. Her eyeshadow matched the dress and she'd used navy liquid liner. The only thing missing was the shoulder pads.

I let out a sigh, well aware that we were quite a sight, and carefully navigated the icy spots on the walkways now that I knew they were there. Rosemarie hovered close by in case she had to sing me back to consciousness, and she let out an audible sigh of relief as I joined her by the yellow Beetle.

"You smell just like my granny did in the nursing home," she said, scrunching her nose. "They used to rub her down with menthol and then cover her in a body sock. She had the softest skin I've ever felt. Made it real hard to have her embalmed after she passed. We ended up having to cremate her. The funeral home director said she lit up like the Fourth of July.

"Come on, I'll drive you to the van." Rosemarie got behind the wheel of the car and I carefully got in the passenger seat, the Icy Hot patches crackling as I moved. The whoosh of menthol surrounded me. "I had to park a couple blocks away and you've got that crazy look in your eye you get when you're on your period. I think you're probably dehydrated and need some lunch. When was the last time you ate?"

"I had rocky road sometime after three and I just drank a cup of coffee while I was taking a shower."

"I've always appreciated your ability to multitask," she said. "I called Mike, by the way. He doesn't normally work on Sundays, but he's coming in special for us. He owes me a favor."

I had the feeling I was about to meet another

one of Rosemarie's conquests. Or at least one of her students from when she was teaching the tantric classes. But she surprised me.

"Mike's daughter was having a lot of trouble in school last year, and I helped get her set up with a tutor. It turns out she's dyslexic. Sixteen years old and no one ever caught it," she said, shaking her head.

"Wow, that's great," I said.

"She's a real sweet kid. Mike would bring her to Whiskey Bayou three days a week for tutoring at the library, and while she was working Mike would pump me like the gas station attendant at the 7-Eleven in one of the back rooms. It was nice while it lasted, but he had no rhythm. It was like being fucked by Mr. Roboto. Never did have an orgasm with him. Pardon my French. I forgot what day it was for a second." She smiled sweetly as she said it, so it took a couple of seconds for that vision to take root.

I wasn't sure what to expect when we pulled into Magic Mike's Auto Shop, but it sure as heck wasn't Mike Winkler. It turns out Mike looked like Vin Diesel on steroids. He wore a pair of gray coveralls zipped halfway up and a tight white t-shirt beneath. I guessed owning a body shop kept a guy in pretty good shape, since I could count at least six abs beneath his shirt. I was guessing there were more, but he'd have to unzip his coveralls a little farther.

"So you're the cunt bitch," he said, looking over the van.

"That's me," I said.

"What's that smell?" he asked, leaning forward to take a couple of sniffs. "Smells just like my Granny. Anytime she got sick she'd rub Vicks all over her chest and the bottom of her feet. Said it worked wonders."

"No idea," I said, arching an eyebrow. Really, the smell couldn't be that noticeable.

He walked off to get his clipboard and I could see what Rosemarie was talking about with the rhythm. My grandfather would've said he had a hitch in his get-along. It was like his hips had been attached to his body Mr. Potato Head style.

He looked over the van, his lips pressed tight together. "They did a bang-up job all right, but it could've been a lot worse. Doesn't look like there's any other damage. You can pick it up in the morning."

I bit my bottom lip. "I've really got to work today. You can't have it done sooner?"

"It'll only take a couple of hours to get it painted, but it needs to dry overnight. Normally, I'd have a loaner you could borrow, but they're all out. Lots of wrecks this week with the weather."

"It's no problem," Rosemarie said. "I'm free the rest of the day to drive her around. We've got a case to work anyway."

"I've got to go to Hilton Head," I told her, thinking *no, no, no* in my head. I was barely functional on my own as a private detective. Adding Rosemarie to the mix had yet to make me feel more competent at my job.

"Like I said, I'm free." Then she turned to look at Mike and batted her lashes. "At least most of the day."

Mike smiled at Rosemarie, the little dimple in his cheek fluttering a bit, and Rosemarie pinkened, her body language changing so her breasts seemed just a little bigger.

"I heard you'd gotten into the crime business part-time," he said. "I hope you're taking care of yourself. It's a real dangerous world out there for a lady like you."

I rolled my eyes so hard I almost fell backward.

"Oh, Mike," she giggled. "You're the sweetest, but you know I can take care of myself. I keep a sawed-off right under the front seat of the car. I'm excellent with a loaded weapon."

"Don't I know it," he said, winking.

I stood there awkwardly while they did some kind of bizarre mating ritual, and then they finally agreed to catch up over drinks later that evening.

We thanked Magic Mike and piled back into the Beetle. "What are you doing?" I asked her. "I thought you said he was like Mr. Roboto in bed."

She chewed on her lip as she took Oglethorpe all the way to the highway and headed toward Hilton Head.

"I know, but he's so damn attractive. Why can't the looks and the sex match up? It's like he was cursed by God or something."

"Maybe he's gotten better since the last time y'all were together. Maybe he doesn't perform well around books."

"I was thinking that same thing," she said. "We've never actually done it in a bed. If all else fails, I can always throw him on his back and ride him like a stallion."

CHAPTER EIGHT

IT WAS A short drive to Hilton Head Island. Our first stop was the Shrimp Shack. Not only so we could grab a bite to eat, but also so we could chat with any workers who might've been on shift when Jonathon Hunt disappeared. But I especially liked the fact that we were getting to eat.

Rosemarie was right. I was dehydrated and needed food. When I didn't eat at regular intervals I'd get a pounding headache and mostly want to kill anyone in sight. Kate called it being hangry.

The Shrimp Shack was located on the beach side of the island, cozily situated between some of the bigger resorts. I wouldn't have called it a shack, exactly. I didn't think they actually allowed shacks on Hilton Head.

The restaurant matched all the other architecture of the area. The siding was painted blue and the windows were trimmed in white. And there were blue-and-white striped awnings that lined the entire front side with tables and chairs beneath them for outdoor seating. Wooden sidewalks with white railings led to all of the little businesses along the waterfront, and docks led down to the water. Boat traffic in this area was as popular as car traffic.

My current look really didn't fit in with the surroundings. I hadn't really thought out my attire as a strategy for the day. I'd been thinking about feeling empowered, especially after the attack the night before. But Rosemarie and I were going to stick out like sore thumbs. This was not an area that embraced the eighties, unless they were watching Dynasty reruns from the comfort of their yachts.

I figured what I was feeling now was how it must feel to be invited to the governor's mansion and then realize once you got there that you weren't wearing any pants. I wasn't sure how Rosemarie was feeling. She was still humming Bohemian Rhapsody under her breath, even though the song had ended twenty minutes ago.

The sun was hidden behind some very un-pleasant looking gray clouds, and it didn't take a weatherman to know a storm was brewing. The wind howled, and Rosemarie's Farrah Fawcett curls whipped around her face in a snarl. Watching her made me wonder why I'd waited thirty years to cut my hair short. I'd made a lot of bad decisions in my life, so it was nice to finally get something right.

The restaurant wasn't crowded. It was the off-season and with the weather the way it was, most of the locals were probably staying close to home. Sometimes storms escalated quickly on the island. Besides, it was getting colder by the minute, which really wasn't pleasant when the Icy Hot patch was on the "icy" round of therapy. My nipples felt like pieces of glass trapped beneath the Band-Aids.

The odd looks we were getting from the occasional local we passed were either caused by our unique clothing combination or the fact that all hell was about to break loose in the sky and they were staring at us in pity. Fishermen and those who dealt with boats had a pretty good handle on the weather, in my experience.

"Wow, these people are real downers," Rosemarie' whispered. "It's like one of those horror movies where the girl stops to buy gas and then she can't find her way out of town. She's trapped there forever, and everyone just stares at her creepily while she panics. Then she finds out it's a town full of zombies and they eat her."

"That story escalated quickly."

"I'm terrified of zombies," Rosemarie confided. "I've got a go-bag in the back of the Beetle in case of the zombie apocalypse. I've got money, food, clothes, and my crossbow in there. And I bought one of those bunkers off the QVC channel. It looks just like a shed in my backyard, but once I flip the switch to seal it off nobody is getting in."

"I think we're going to be fine," I assured her, though I was secretly intrigued about the bunker. "I'm sure they're just surprised to see us."

We made our way down the long boardwalk until we got to the Shrimp Shack. An older man with salt-and-pepper hair and a swarthy complex-ion moved to greet us, and then he seemed perplexed as he got a full look at the two of us standing there. I could sympathize. He seemed to catch himself and then welcomed us.

"I'm Emilio and this is my place," he said, leading us to a table near the window. "It's slow today, but we're offering the full menu. Unless the storm blows in earlier than expected and then it's every man for himself."

"Good to know," I said.

"Where are you ladies from?" he asked.

"Savannah," Rosemarie said. "And I'm starving. They did communion at church this morning, but those little crackers only make you hungrier. The lady in front of me asked the guy next to her if he was going to eat his. I thought she was going to snatch it right out of his hand."

We ordered, but before Emilio could take our menus I introduced myself. "My name is Addison Holmes," I said, passing him a card. "We're actually here investigating the death of Jonathon Hunt."

He looked at my card and then nodded. "The police questioned all of us," he said. "The Hunts were regulars, even in the off-season. It was a terrible thing that happened to him. They never caught who did it?"

"No, they didn't," I said.

"You should let him rest in peace. It only brings pain to the family. They're here on the island now. Why would you keep digging?"

I knew the family was in town, which was one

of the reasons I wanted to come and check things out myself. The Hunt family was booked on a flight to Paris tomorrow. It was my only window of opportunity to talk to Mrs. Hunt in person.

"Because what happened to Mr. Hunt has happened to another man," I told him. "And it could keep happening. I've been hired by a private party to see if I can dig up any more information on the case. Mr. Hunt wasn't a random target of violence. He wasn't robbed. He was specifically selected to have his heart taken from him. Just like the other man in Savannah."

"And you think you can find out things the police can't?" he asked, arching a brow skeptically.

"I'm not tied down by as many rules, and having a private client gives me more freedom. To come across state lines, for example, and connect the two victims."

He sighed and said, "Let me put in your order and I'll sit and talk with you a bit. I like the looks of you. You look honest. Like that actress."

"Liza Minnelli?" I asked, thinking of Rosemarie's earlier comment.

He looked startled. "No. But one of you smells a little like her. She used to perform over at The

Jazz Corner, and she'd stop in here occasionally."

Rosemarie stared at me as if waiting for me to claim the Icy Hot smell, but I just stayed silent. All I knew was my body didn't hurt quite as bad as it probably should have, and my sinuses were really clear.

We waited a good twenty minutes for him to get things settled with the restaurant, and when he came back over to the table he was carrying Rosemarie's fried shrimp basket and my crab bisque and salad. Emilio grabbed a chair from another table and pulled it up to ours, seating himself at the end of the table.

"You were here the day Jonathon disappeared?" I asked. I took a sip of the soup and wanted to roll my eyes back into my head it was so good.

"I was here, and I spoke to him several times. Like I said, they're regulars and have been for more than ten years. Their daughter had her graduation party here last year."

"He seemed in good spirits that day?"

"Oh, yes. It was high season and he'd just purchased his first yacht. He was very proud of it. They docked it right out there and all came up to the restaurant laughing," he said, pointing out to one of the docks. "The oldest daughter had a boyfriend with her, but he was a regular as well. Families on this island tend to stick together." He shrugged as if it was a given.

I knew that to be a fact in this part of the country. Money associated with money. It was one of the many reasons Nick's parents hated me.

"They came in and sat at one of the round tables in the corner," he said, pointing to the back. "They'd called ahead and made reservations, so we'd been expecting them. Locals always get priority seating."

"Did Mr. Hunt order a drink from the bar?" I asked.

"He did," Emilio said, nodding. "He ordered an Old Fashioned, just like always."

"The coroner found bourbon in his system along with GHB."

"The date rape drug?" he asked, confused.

"They needed to get him to the bathroom. If he was ill and disoriented it wouldn't have been difficult to get him out the window. We walked around the building before we came in. The area behind the building is where the dumpsters are.

I'm assuming it's not a high traffic area."

Emilio was looking a little sick now. "No. In fact, there are no trespassing signs posted. With more and more tourists on the island, we started having fights back there and a little drug trade, so the police put the signs up."

"Do you remember who gave him the drink?" I asked.

"Actually, I did," he said, blowing out a breath and leaning back in his chair. "This is my place, and I take that seriously. When things get busy I make myself useful—deliver food, answer the phone, seat guests, deal with troublemakers." He shrugged a shoulder. "But I also enjoy getting to know my customers and their families. I took the drink to Jonathon so I could visit for a few minutes. This is a family place. My ex-wife and I opened in more than twenty years ago."

"Is your ex-wife still part-owner?" Rosemarie asked.

"Nah, she owns The Salty Oyster on the other side of the island. It turns out we get along better if we never see each other."

"Who made the drink?" I asked.

"Look, my place has an impeccable reputation.

Everyone that works here full-time has been with me for years. I hire seasonal help in the summer, but they're just college kids on break. I don't want rumors started."

"The police didn't ask you these questions after the murder?" I asked, surprised.

"Of course not. We're not suspects. The police here know better than to ask questions like that to some of the families on this island. They'd be out of a job. As far as I know, they were only looking at outsiders."

"I don't believe you or your workers had anything to do with Mr. Hunt's death, unless you happen to have a waiter that moonlights as a surgeon. Whoever killed Mr. Hunt was skilled. But the fact remains that someone drugged his drink between the time it took the bartender to make the drink and when you brought it to the table."

Emilio looked thoughtful for a few minutes, and I wondered if he was going to get up and leave. Rosemarie had been blessedly silent. She was making her way through a mound of fried shrimp and I wasn't even sure she was listening all that closely to the conversation. I was really starting to feel like I had a handle on things. Maybe I was going to make a good P.I. after all.

"In high season everything is chaos," Emilio said. "Especially at the bar. Things get backed up sometimes as orders come in, but they work a pretty efficient system. The trays are lined up along the bar and the ticket is there with the table number and drink order. Jason fills them as he goes."

"But the drinks might sit there a few minutes, depending on how long it takes him to fill the order and how busy the wait staff is?" I asked.

"Exactly," Emilio said. "But if it's too long the ice will melt and he'll have to make a new drink. I'd say no more than ten minutes, tops. But probably less than that for someone like Mr. Hunt. The tickets with local families are marked with a star and given priority."

"Is the bar area usually pretty crowded?"

"Everywhere in here is crowded during high season. People might come to eat, or just for happy hour to cool off after a day on the water. The bar is usually three deep. It's hard for the wait staff to move in and out of the crowd with the trays. It's not an easy job."

"I waited tables in college," I said. "I remember those days without fondness."

Emilio smiled. "It's not for everyone."

"What about when Mr. Hunt got up to go to the bathroom."

"When Jonathon didn't return from the restroom, Eloise asked if I'd go in and check on him. She said he hadn't been feeling well. I'd seen that for myself as he'd passed me on the way. I asked if he was all right, but he just nodded and kept going rather quickly. He bumped into a woman coming out of the other restroom, and she seemed a bit perturbed he didn't apologize."

"Did you know the woman?"

"No, but I'll never forget her. She's probably one of the most beautiful women I've ever seen. I immediately went to her after Jonathon bumped into her to smooth things over. She looked like she was going to follow him into the bathroom and give him a piece of her mind. I love Southern temper in a woman," he said with a grin. "Except my ex-wife. I didn't enjoy it that much with her."

"Can you describe the woman?" I asked.

"Of course. The memory of her is etched on my brain. She looked like Wonder Woman." I'm not sure what the look on my face was, but it must've told him he'd said something important. "Not Lynda Carter. The new one," he said, nodding. "She was probably young enough to be my daughter, maybe twenty-eight or thirty years old, but I would've asked her out if I could've found her again."

"She left right then?" I asked him.

"I don't think so. She thanked me for explaining to her about Jonathon and then she said her friends were waiting for her. Someone dropped a drink in the bar at that point and I had to go make sure no one stepped on any glass. By the time I thought to look for her again, she was gone."

It wasn't a lot to go on, since I had no clue who the Wonder Woman lookalike was, but I didn't believe in coincidences.

We thanked Emilio for his time and paid our tab, and I tried not to have a panic attack when I saw the total. I needed to stick to takeout Chinese. Island prices were out of my budget.

CHAPTER NINE

WE MADE A quick stop at the Beach Comber Inn, where Jonathon Hunt's body had been discovered. Unfortunately, the hotel didn't retain employees like the Shrimp Shack. Almost an entirely new staff had been hired since last summer.

We did talk to the manager, who was completely unhelpful and didn't care for the fact that we were talking in his lobby about the body that had been found in one of his hotel rooms. I could kind of see his point, but he was such a dislikable fellow I couldn't really work up the effort to care.

Fredrick Hinkle was his name, and he'd looked to be a healthy mix of both Alfred Hitchcock and Don Rickles. It was a face I assumed only his mother could love, which, in turn, was why he was such a hateful little man. His head was bald and shined to mirror-like perfection and he had the body of Humpty Dumpty.

After speaking with Fredrick Hinkle for five minutes I could understand why there was such a huge staff turnover. We hadn't gleaned one new piece of information from him, and I might have accidentally stepped on his toe when he asked us if we shopped out of the missionary barrel.

Things devolved pretty quickly from that point, so we made our leave and headed to our last stop. The good news was Hinkle hadn't made one comment about the smell of Icy Hot, though as he'd been talking to us he kept pinching the tip of his nose and backing away. The bad news was I was pretty sure I was going to have to have my leather jacket professionally cleaned to get the smell of grandmothers out.

Hilton Head Island was kind of shaped like a giant incisor, and the Hunts had a home at the bottommost point of the tooth. Thick copses of trees divided property lines of the enormous homes along the coast, and they were bending with the wind as the storm blew closer. We wouldn't have long with Mrs. Hunt, if she'd talk to us at all, before we needed to get off the island.

I'd run a background check on Eloise Hunt

back at the agency. She'd grown up in Asheville, North Carolina, the oldest of four girls, and the daughter of two teachers. She hadn't come from money, and from what I could find, she seemed like a very down-to-earth lady.

Eloise had taught in the public school system when she and Jonathon were first married up until she'd had her first child, then decided to stay home with the children, both of whom seemed to be bright students and non-assholes (which was really the most you could ask for in today's society). She'd started volunteering once the kids got older, and since her husband's death she'd created the Jonathon Hunt Education Foundation for under-privileged students who showed promise in the maths and sciences.

We followed the GPS directions and took a left, splitting away from the other majestic homes, and my eyes nearly fell out of my head when the Hunt's home came into view. The house looked like a palace. A big white palace. And it was on an inlet, so the front and back both had an ocean view. Palms trees had been planted around the grounds, but they'd also left the natural trees of the area standing, so it looked part rainforest.

It was three floors of terraces and windows, so any room in the house showed what I was guessing was a spectacular view of the ocean. The yacht Mr. Hunt had been so proud of was tied to the dock, and a tennis court was off to the side. A swimming pool that was almost the length of the house shimmered cerulean between the house and the darker blue-green of the ocean.

Rosemarie drove the car along the circular drive toward the front of the house, and I saw Eloise Hunt standing on the porch waiting for us. She gave a wave and a motion for us to park under the covered portico. I was guessing Emilio had called to give her a heads-up about our arrival.

"I tell you what," Rosemarie said, gaping like a tourist. "I could learn to live like this. How long do you think it takes to acclimate to living the life of luxury? I always wondered what it must be like to be able to afford the organic milk instead of the cheap stuff that makes men develop breasts."

"Maybe you should become a broker instead of a choir teacher."

"I'll give it some serious thought. I read that people often make major career moves the closer they get to forty."

"I thought you loved teaching," I said, surprised.

"Oh, I do. But I find that I've started looking forward to summer a lot sooner in the year the longer I teach."

"I think that's normal. I used to do that too."

"Probably not on the second day of school though."

She parked the car under the portico and turned to look at me, her hand on the door handle. "I can hardly smell that Icy Hot now that the inside of my nostrils are singed from the smell. I've never experienced the strength of an aroma like that. I bet if I lit a match we'd both go up in flames. How many of those patches did you put on?"

"I don't know," I shrugged. "Maybe six or seven. I was working with the old 'an ounce of prevention' adage. I'm tired of my body hurting, so I figured I'd stay ahead of the pain."

"How's your head?"

"I could probably use another dose of painkillers and a nap."

"Someone told me an orgasm is as good as a painkiller for a headache. It releases all those endorphins and it makes you sleepy, so you'll be primed for a nap immediately following."

"I'll stick with the painkillers for the moment. Probably Mrs. Hunt has had enough trauma in her life without finding me with my pants down, curled up asleep like a cat on her bathroom rug."

"I guess if you put it that way," Rosemarie said.

We got out of the car and Mrs. Hunt walked toward us with her hand outstretched to shake mine. "You must be Addison Holmes. Emilio told me you'd probably stop by."

"Thank you so much for seeing us, Mrs. Hunt. We won't take much of your time."

She turned and smiled at Rosemarie and said, "Y'all can call me Eloise. Better come in before the rain starts."

She had a charming Southern accent, different from those of us who lived in Georgia, but she immediately made me feel at home. Everything about her was delicate. Not fragile. But whereas some people were painted in bold strokes of color, Eloise was a watercolor. Her hair was a soft blonde and waved around her heart-shaped face, and her eyes were misty blue. She wore a long-sleeved caftan in swirling shades of blue that looked immensely comfortable, and it was belted with a yellow sash.

I wasn't going to lie. I wanted that caftan. Which brought up a major concern because I never thought I'd reach the age where I openly coveted a caftan.

"I made some hot tea and put it out on the veranda," she continued as we made our way up a sweeping double staircase that led to the second story. "There's a bitter chill in the air today."

"I want that caftan so bad," Rosemarie whispered.

"I'm getting one," I whispered back. "I might never wear anything else. It's like a fancy bathrobe."

The veranda was a covered space and heat lamps lined the perimeter to ward off the cold. It was screened in and the floor was a stained concrete complete with fleur de lis designs in a darker stain. It looked very expensive and so polished it could've been wood. White wicker furniture with white cushions made it look like an outdoor living room, and I wondered how hard it was to keep all that white clean.

"I always enjoy sitting out here and watching the storms roll in," she said. "And the kids are around and about in the house, and I figure they don't need to hear what we're going to talk about. Jon's death has hit my son especially hard. He just turned sixteen. They were very close."

"I'm so sorry for your loss," I told her, taking a seat in one of the chairs. "From everything I've read about your husband, he was an incredible man."

"Oh, he was," she agreed, smiling, the lines of grief on her face disappearing for just a moment.

When she said she'd made tea, what she really meant was that she'd made *tea*. The service sat on the glass coffee table, complete with brown and white sugar cubes and milk. But next to the tea service was a three-tiered plate with tiny cakes and sandwiches overflowing. I kind of wanted her to adopt me.

"People were constantly trying to get Jon into politics," she said. "They'd say he was just the kind of man this country needed. But he was never interested. He always said he could do a lot more good donating money directly to those that needed it rather than spending all his time fundraising with all that money going toward trying to get re-elected."

"We don't want to take up a lot of your time, but I'm sure Emilio told you that what happened to your husband has also happened to another man."

"Yes, he did," she nodded. "That's why I wanted to see you. I'll help however I can. That day is still such a blur. Everything happened so fast. One minute he was sitting beside me and the next he was gone. And then I was planning his funeral and trying to figure out how to comfort two grieving children. It took a couple of weeks for it to all catch up with me so I could grieve too."

I took a long sip of tea to keep from bursting into tears on the spot. I didn't do well in situations like this one. I was a sympathetic crier, and I'd already heard Rosemarie sniffle once. Eloise was dry-eyed, but she looked as if the tears might start at any moment.

I cleared my throat. "We believe your husband and the other victim were specifically targeted because of their blood type. They were both O-negative, which is rare, and it makes it very difficult for organ donors to be found since the blood type has to match."

"Yes, Jon always made it a point to donate blood regularly because of that. In fact, he was a little annoyed, because the last time he had to give blood he ended up on all kinds of third party lists and was getting phone calls all the time asking if he'd either donate more blood or consider becoming a kidney donor."

"Any specific company?" I asked.

"Not that I know of. It's just like with anything. Once you donate once they'll hound you for the rest of your life."

"They found GHB in your husband's system."

"That's what the police told me," she said, clasping her hands together on her lap. "That he'd been drugged to get him out of the restaurant, but it was impossible to know who'd done it.

"Or *why* they'd done it. So many people knew and loved Jon. At least the locals. I could never make sense of it before. The why," she said, her hands clasping together tighter until her knuckles turned white. "But to know he was targeted from the beginning. That someone came to the island for the express purpose of killing him is *unconscionable*. If they'd only known him. They never would have chosen him. He was such a good man."

"Emilio mentioned a woman your husband ran into on the way to the bathroom. Did you happen to see her?"

"No," she said, shrugging. "Our table didn't really have a good view of the bathrooms. I watched him walk away and that's the last time I ever saw him alive." Her words hitched once and a single tear spilled over. That had been it for me.

We excused ourselves quickly and by the time we got back in the car we were both crying.

"I need some wine," Rosemarie said. "And some eye pads. I can't see Magic Mike looking like this."

She was right. Rosemarie looked a bit...startling. Her hair was rather snarled and tall and her navy eye makeup had smudged under her eyes. She would've fit right in on the set of Bee-tlejuice.

What I needed was some alone time to de-compress. I missed living in a house. I missed watching comfort movies while drinking wine and crying by myself. Crying was a great stress reliever.

Rosemarie took a paper napkin out of her bag

and wrapped up inside it was a few of the tea cakes.

"You had a look," she said.

"Thank you." And then I shoved one of the cakes in my mouth.

CHAPTER TEN

Monday

WHEN I WOKE up the next morning I felt like I'd been run over by a truck. A really big truck. My neck was sore due to the fact that I'd fallen asleep half sitting up. The front of my pajamas held the remnants of popcorn kernels and my iPad was still propped against the wall.

After Rosemarie had dropped me at the agency, I'd decided to call it a day. Rosemarie had left in a hurry so she could get ready for her date with Magic Mike, and I'd made popcorn and settled in on my mattress to watch Netflix for the rest of the night. I'd also peeled off my old Icy Hot patches and applied new ones. The bruises hadn't disappeared. I needed to visit Chermaine and have her rub whatever cream she'd put on Scarlet's face on my body.

I wasn't sure what time it was, but when I

looked at my phone I noticed Nick had called twice and my mother had called three times. I decided it was best not to return either of them at the moment. I needed to get presentable and get to work. And I needed to pick up my van.

There was a knock at the door and Kate stuck her head in. She jumped at the sight of me. "Holy shit," she said, slapping a hand to her chest as she caught her breath. "You scared the hell out of me. You look like one of those marionettes just propped up against the wall. You know how much dolls creep me out. Have you looked at yourself in the mirror?"

"I did yesterday. I wasn't that impressed. I've decided to start wearing caftans though."

"Seems like an interesting move." Kate closed the door to the office and sat in the chair behind my desk. "Why does it smell like my granny in here?"

"Why does everyone's granny smell the same? Why can't grannies smell like apple spice or a fresh baked chicken?"

"Are you drunk?"

"I don't think so," I said. "I didn't buy the boxed wine at Walgreen's the other night."

"Probably a wise decision," Kate said. "I like your hair, by the way. Want to tell me why your eyes are swollen and you're covered in bruises? I'm assuming that's where the old lady smell is coming from. How many of those patches do you have on?"

"All of them that were left in the box." And then I broke down and told her about sleeping with Nick, my stakeout at the Tiger Lounge, being a cunt bitch, and the trip to Hilton Head. "And I put Band-Aids on my nipples yesterday instead of wearing a bra, and now I can't get them off."

"You had a busy weekend. I had to spend mine with my in-laws."

"We should trade next time," I said. I liked Kate's in-laws.

"My suggestion is that you take several pain killers, get in the shower and rinse of the popcorn kernels, forget about Nick for at least the next twenty-four hours, and get to work on the Dunnegan case. The weather has cleared up and the longer you sit there the stiffer you're going to get."

"I don't think I like those suggestions. You have any more?"

"Sure, call your mom back. You'll probably

feel much better when you get off the phone with her."

"You're a horrible bitch," I said.

She grinned. "I know. Now get up. Looking at you is depressing the hell out of me. I've told you a million times you can stay in my guest bedroom. You don't have to keep sleeping here."

"I know, and I appreciate the offer. But I don't want to impose on you guys. I know Mike is a free-range husband."

Mike McClean was a big, Scottish, teddy bear of a man. He was solid as a rock, at least six foot five, and he had a shock of red hair. He was still a cop for the Savannah PD, and a couple of months ago we'd found out that he had a bit of a gambling addiction. He and Kate were still working through all that, and I didn't want to interfere. Besides, Mike really *was* a free-range husband. He hated wearing clothes when he was home.

"The offer always stands," she said, getting up and opening the door. "Oh, and be careful messing around too much with Ugly Mo. That could turn out to be bad business all around."

"No kidding. Especially for the cunt bitch."

I DID FEEL better after a shower and pain killers. I wasn't a hundred percent, and if anyone saw me naked they'd probably run screaming in the opposite direction, but I was able to hold my own as long as I didn't have to chase anyone down or get into a physical altercation. I figured it was a fifty-fifty chance.

I dressed in yoga pants and a sweatshirt, since denim hurt the bruises on my hips, and I put on socks and tennis shoes. Since it was a possibility the van had become a target, I decided not to take any chances. I Velcroed my elastic holster around my waist and transferred my gun from my purse, and then I pulled my sweatshirt down to cover it.

I needed to follow up with Anthony Dunnegan, and then I was hitting the streets. The sooner I put this case to rest, the less likely I was to stab Anthony in the eye with a fork.

I used the phone number he'd given us in the file.

"Mr. Dunnegan," I said when he answered. "This is Addison Holmes."

"Baby, I told you not to call me at this number. You've got to use the other line."

"Actually, you *did* tell me to use this number.

And don't call me baby. I'm the private investigator looking for your missing kidney."

"Oh, right. Nurse Ratchet. I ought to sue you for dumping me in that room after I passed out. I didn't know where the hell I was when I woke up."

"You're welcome to sue, but I figure you don't want the hassle, since you sexually harassed me in front of witnesses while you were under the influence of drugs," I lied without any remorse whatsoever.

"Whatever. Everyone knows suits like that are best bought off with a settlement. How much do you want?"

"How about we get down to business."

"Whatever," he said. "I've got plans tonight, so hurry it up."

"Hopefully it involves a church and a lot of rosaries." Since it was barely eight o'clock in the morning, I'd apparently made the wrong assumption that he was at work.

"I'll be seeing God, if that's what you're asking."

"I wasn't," I said dryly. "When was the last time you gave blood?" I asked.

"I'm unable to give blood," he said.

"I didn't see anything in your medical report from the hospital," I said. "Do you have a condition?"

"I'm healthy. I just don't like doing it, which makes me unable."

I opened my mouth to say something, but snapped it shut. It was one of those moments where silence was the better option.

"I believe you were targeted because of your blood type. Did you know you were O-negative?"

"Sure," he said. "I got the report back after our life insurance applications were accepted. They sent some nurse out to the house to do a medical workup. She took blood too. Hot little thing. Tried calling the cell number she put down on the forms, but she never called me back. Prick tease."

I disconnected and felt the need to shower again. Instead, I grabbed my bag and headed out. I caught Jimmy Royal as he was coming into work.

"Just the man I want to see," I said. "I need a ride to pick up my van."

"No can do. One trip to that neighborhood was enough for me. My business with Ugly Mo is concluded."

I narrowed my eyes. "Yeah, that would've been

helpful information before you sent *me* down there."

He smiled and put his hands up in surrender. "Hey, I was simply passing along information. What you did with it was your business. Everyone knows Ugly Mo in this area. I figured you knew the risk."

"Funny, because I'd never heard of him. But now I've been roped into following his wife to see if she's tearing up the sheets and trading secrets to his competitor."

Jimmy paled. "Holy shit. You want to stay far away from Fat Louie. That guy is nothing but trouble. Even the cops give him a wide berth. Word on the street is he killed his own mother. They found her in her bathtub with her wrists cut, but she had a couple of defensive wounds. The rumor was she'd been Louie's bookkeeper and had been cooking two sets of books, siphoning off money for herself. But she'd also been working with the IRS to get him on tax evasion. The ultimate double cross. Send your son to prison and keep his empire. Then she died and it all went away."

"If I end up with my wrists cut I'm going to

haunt you for the rest of your life," I told him.

"I wouldn't worry about that," Jimmy said. "Louie's MO is a nice clean slice right across the throat."

I thought about it for a second and remembered the words on my would-be attacker's cheek. And then I thunked myself in the head. "I'm assuming if I run into a guy with the words 'Property of FL' tattooed on their body that they work for Fat Louie?"

"Yep. He brands the entire gang for two reasons. It's a warning to everyone else not to fuck with his people. And it guarantees that his people will never be able to work for anyone else."

"Great," I said. "So my brand new van that I bought from Ugly Mo has now been targeted by his biggest enemy. One of his henchmen stopped by the agency the other night and practiced spelling some new words on the sides of the van. It's at the auto shop being repainted now. Which is where you're going to drop me." I smiled and he backed up another step. I really wasn't happy with Jimmy Royal at the moment. "It's the least you can do."

JIMMY DROPPED ME off at Magic Mike's and drove off without waiting to see if the van was ready.

A guy came out of the garage dressed in a pair of coveralls similar to the ones Mike had been wearing the day before. The only difference was the name Joe was embroidered over the front right pocket.

"Good Lord," I said before I could help myself. This guy was even better looking and more muscled than Magic Mike.

"Are you Addison Holmes?" he asked.

"Did my Aunt Scarlet set this up?" I crossed my arms over my chest and took a step back, looking around to see if there were cameras or anything like that. I expected loud, thumping music to start at any moment and for Joe to begin his strip tease.

"I beg your pardon?"

"Uh huh," I said skeptically. "I'm just saying the gesture is nice, but I really don't have time for any funny business this morning. Besides, I'm trying to decide if I should accept a marriage proposal, and though I'm not really sure if I'm actually in a relationship right now since we had a fight the other night, it makes my stomach feel a little squishy to partake in something like this."

"Are you one of those over-sharers?" he asked.

"Only when I'm nervous. I don't have any dollar bills on me. But you seem very nice."

He looked at me a little strangely and said, "Mike threw his back out last night, but he called this morning and said to tell you there's no charge for the paint job. The keys are under the visor." Joe turned and went back into the garage, whistling between his teeth.

I stood there a full minute before I realized that Magic Mike's was not a body shop/strip club. It was just a body shop.

"All righty then," I said to no one. "Moving along."

CHAPTER ELEVEN

'D JUST PULLED away from Magic Mike's when my cell phone rang. I saw Scarlet's number flash across the screen and answered.

"Swing by and pick me up," she said. "I've got an inside track on all this black market organ business. And I wouldn't mind picking up a donut. They keep trying to feed me eggs here. I hate eggs."

"I can be there in five minutes," I told her and disconnected. I turned on the next one-way street and headed toward East Oglethorpe.

When I pulled up to The Ballastone my eyebrows raised so far up my eyelids felt stretched. Aunt Scarlet and Ugly Mo were standing next to the bellman, talking animatedly with each other.

Scarlet had on a pair of black leggings and an oversized men's white dress shirt. Her top button was undone and she was wearing her three-strand pearl necklace and matching earrings. She still had on her white tennis shoes with the blades in the toes and her fur coat was draped over her shoulders.

Mo was wearing another three-piece suit, this one black with silver pinstripes. He had on a fedora and was carrying a different cane today, this one with an engraved silver handle that matched the pinstripes in his suit.

I stopped the van in front of them and unlocked the doors. They both chose to get in the black leather swivel chairs in the back.

"You remember Ugly Mo?" Aunt Scarlet asked.

"I sure do," I said. The biggest question on my mind was why he was in my van. "How's it going, Mo?"

"I'm doing all right. Little arthritis in my neck, but we smoked a real nice blend this morning, so it's feeling better."

"You two met up this morning to smoke weed?" I asked. I turned in the seat to look at them. Scarlet's face was nice and relaxed and she was looking at Mo with a dreamy look in her eyes. Mo hadn't stopped grinning since he got in the car.

"Nah, we met up last night," Scarlet said. "We exchanged numbers when he hired us for the case, and all of a sudden last night I hear a little ding on my phone and it was Mo. Then one thing led to another and we started sexting. I'm a real creative sexter, so Mo sent me a picture of his penis. I understand that's how it's done now."

It was fortunate I was stopped at a red light. I thunked my head on the wheel once and then once more for good measure.

"Can you believe in ninety years of living I've never seen a black man's penis?"

I wheezed in a deep breath and went into a fit of coughing. Scarlet leaned up and slapped me on the back a couple of times and then the light turned green and I moved forward with the other traffic.

"I was surprised too," she said. "I've seen Chinese, Korean, Australian, British, Indian, and Iranian. And American of course, but you get bored with those after a while," she whispered like she was sharing national secrets. "But in all that time I've never seen a black one. So I told Mo to come on over because I wanted to see it in person.

Now I know why he walks with a cane. It's like having an anaconda in your pants. Can put you off balance for sure."

Mo laughed and he and Scarlet knuckle bumped. "Once you go black, baby, you'll never go back."

"I'd always wondered what that saying meant," Scarlet said.

I didn't know how old Ugly Mo was. Maybe somewhere between forty and seventy. It was hard to tell because of the disfigurement of his face. But however old he was, he was still a heck of a lot younger than Scarlet.

"Aunt Scarlet, he's married!" I said, giving both of them a disapproving look.

I was heading for the donut shop and nobody was going to stop me.

Mo waved his hand in dismissal. "Jasmine's always had a bit of a wayward pussy. I never minded none. I got a business to run. Nobody got time for a high maintenance ho like Jasmine full-time. It's best she spread herself among the brothers, if you get my drift."

Scarlet started to giggle and then Mo joined her. I had two high senior citizens in my van. And worse than that, Mo was one of the passengers. If Fat Louie's henchmen saw me driving Mo around they'd come after me with a vengeance.

"Why am I following her if you know she's cheating?" I asked.

"I don't care about the cheating," he said. "I care about her running her yap to Fat Louie. I don't got time for her alive, but I got even less time for her dead. There's all kinds of shit you gotta do when someone dies. I'm a busy man. Besides, you seen the titties on that woman? Ain't no coffin gonna hold those. Have to have one special made. That shit's expensive."

"I always wanted titties like that," Scarlet said. "Maybe I'll buy some."

"No, girl," Mo said, patting her thigh. "Your titties are just fine once you find them."

"Kill me now," I said and turned into the drive-thru for the donut shop. The line was long, but we moved through pretty quickly. By the time I got to the window to order I was feeling a little like Michael Douglas in that movie where he went batshit crazy and started bashing everyone's car window's in with a baseball bat.

I ordered a dozen assorted for Mo and Scarlet,

and a chocolate eclair, a bear claw, and an apple fritter for myself. I needed specialty donuts. And a large black coffee.

I figured the safest thing to do was change the subject. "What kind of insider information do you have about the black market organ transplants?" I asked.

"That's why I called you. Ugly Mo knows all about that black market stuff," Scarlet said.

"That's true," Mo chimed in. "I deal in black market everything. Even groceries. You want me to sign you up for our grocery box service? You pay a monthly club fee and then you get a box of groceries delivered to your door once a week. Whatever is in the box is what you get. Depends on what the trucks are delivering and how accessible they are, if you get my meaning. It's a real popular service."

"How much is it?" I asked. I was kind of interested. I was living on a budget, and I hated to go to the grocery store.

"Hundred bucks a month. But I'll give you the family discount since you're Miss Scarlet's niece."

"Okay," I agreed. "You hear what happened to Anthony Dunnegan?"

Mo laughed and slapped the top of his thigh. "Sure did. Everybody hates that dude. Nobody gonna care if some shyster lawyer gets his kidney stolen. It's a damn shame they didn't take something more permanent, know what I'm saying?"

"Actually, I do," I said. That was one of those injustices of the world, that a man like Jonathon Hunt was killed, but Anthony Dunnegan was left to keep wreaking havoc on the world. "What about a guy named Jonathon Hunt?" I asked. "He had his heart taken while on vacation in Hilton Head."

"Don't know nothing about that," Mo said. "But I know about a lady up in Atlanta that was killed a few years back. That's when the talk first started, so it's been going on a while. Word is they're looking for rare donors and hunt them down. The asshole lawyer and the other dude, they got anything in common?"

"Both O-negative blood type," I said. "Both white males over the age of forty. Each married with a couple of kids. And both are wealthy. What did they take from the woman in Atlanta?" I asked.

"Heart," he said. "Every once in a while, Ugly Mo will get a client that needs something special.

I'm like a broker, you might say. I take a small upfront fee and then put people together to make the magic happen. But those kinds of deals are rare," he said, shrugging. "Not everybody gonna need a hard-to-get organ, but those donor lists are long and people will pay big bucks to get theirs before anyone else."

"What kind of big bucks?" I asked, finishing off my second pastry.

"Depends on which organ. A kidney's going to go for less than a heart or lungs. But prices start at a quarter of a mil."

"Holy cow," I said. "That's steep."

"That's the cost of livin'," he said with a shrug.

"Not everyone can afford those kinds of prices," I said.

"Black market is black market for a reason, no matter what the product. People from the projects ain't the clients. Gotta have money to even get a whiff of who to contact for those kinds of services. And there's hardly ever direct contact. People gotta use brokers like me. It's a delicate business."

"Good point," I said.

"Where are we heading?" Scarlet asked. "We're free until this afternoon, so we can give you a little added muscle. It's not every P.I. that gets the combined experience the two of us come with. We're a real asset."

I smiled and finished my third pastry. "We're going to the Olde Pink House," I told them. "I want to see if anyone remembers the woman that lured in Anthony Dunnegan."

"Girl, you ain't going to find these people. They're long gone by now. Like smoke. Can't even get in touch with them the same way each time. You have to wait for them to contact you."

"Well, shit," I said.

"Pretty much," Mo agreed.

CHAPTER TWELVE

THE OLDE PINK House was, in fact, an old pink house.

It was on the corner of Abercorn and East Bryan, and directly across from Reynolds Square. It was a little after ten o'clock, so the restaurant wasn't open for business yet and there were parking places available street side. I chose an empty side of the street and took up two parking spots.

"If we stay long enough they'll be open for lunch," Scarlet said. "I could really go for a chicken pot pie."

"You just had a whole box of donuts!" I said.

"It's the munchies. That medicinal marijuana really kick starts the appetite."

I tried not to think what the three of us looked like as we approached the front doors of the restaurant. If I was inside and saw us coming, I'd lock the doors. But when I pulled on the handle it came right open.

It was quiet inside, and voices came from the direction of the kitchen along with something that smelled delicious. I guess it wouldn't hurt to have lunch if we were still here when they opened.

There was a young girl at the front dressed in black pants and a crisply pressed white dress shirt. She had on a bowtie and her blonde hair was neatly braided and hung over one shoulder.

"I'm sorry, but we're not open for lunch yet," she said with a smile.

"I just need to speak to the manager," I told her.

She shot a wide-eyed look at Scarlet and Mo and then hurried back to the kitchen area. A few minutes later a man approached us and held out his hand for an introduction. He looked pressed for time and a little annoyed to be interrupted, but he smiled and held out his hand to shake mine.

"I'm Richard Drake," he said. "Lisa said you wanted to speak to the manager."

And then he saw Mo standing behind me.

"Mo," the manager said with a grin. He let go of my head and went to shake Mo's, slapping him on the shoulder in greeting. "I wasn't expecting you today. The hostess didn't know it was you. This is her second day. We're trying her out on the lunch shift so she can get the hang of things. We can go ahead and seat you for lunch."

Ugly Mo gave him a beaming smile. "We'd love that, Rich," Mo said. "My lady friend has her sights set on some chicken pot pie. This is Scarlet Holmes and her niece Addison," Mo said introducing us. "Addison here is a private investigator and she's following a few leads. She needs to talk to you a bit, and then we'll be happy to stay for lunch."

"Of course," Richard said. "Whatever you need. Let me get a table set up and we'll get comfortable."

Richard left us in the entryway to get things set up for early lunch visitors and I stood there, goggling at the difference in Mo's demeanor.

"What's up with the fancy talk?" I whispered.

Mo grinned. "That's why I'm successful, girl. You gotta know your mark. I can't talk to a brother in my neighborhood like that. He'd laugh his ass off. And I can't talk to Rich like a brother. He wouldn't be setting up a table for us right now if I did. But Mo keeps relationships with all kinds of people, because you never know when someone might owe you a favor or two."

"That's wisdom right there," Scarlet said. "Us Holmes women like to leap before we look. It's in the blood. And we almost always land on our feet. Except for my great grandmother, who was pushed from the sixth floor of the Cosmopolitan Hotel by her husband when he discovered her in bed with his business partner. She landed smack on her head."

That story always gave me the heebie-jeebies. I'd seen pictures of Abigail Holmes. She looked a heck of a lot like I did.

We settled in at a table near the fireplace and Richard Drake joined us. From out of nowhere goblets of water appeared and Ugly Mo had a Whiskey Sour in his hand. I had to give him props for being able to drink like that before eleven in the morning. Freshly baked cornbread muffins and butter were put in the center of the table, and the donuts I'd just eaten magically disappeared as my appetite came back.

"Are you acquainted with Anthony Dunnegan?" I asked Richard, while slathering one of the muffins with butter.

"I'm acquainted with his firm," Richard said. "All of the partners use this restaurant frequently for lunch and dinner meetings. They actually have an expense account set up with us."

"He was here for dinner Friday before last," I told him.

"Sure, I remember him coming in. He met with a couple of clients here in the dining area. I remember because Anthony showed up about fifteen till six, but the ladies he met didn't show until almost six-thirty. I wouldn't have known, but he was angry about his clients and said some very inappropriate things to his waitress. He'd also been drinking a bit, so that contributed."

I couldn't say I was surprised to hear it.

"The waitress came back into the kitchen crying, so I went out to speak with Mr. Dunnegan to see what the problem was. What it comes down to is that he's just an impolite, distasteful man. I was polite to him because I knew he'd make a scene if I said what I really wanted to, and his clients finally came in about that time, so I left it alone. But the next morning I called the firm and talked directly with Craig Capshaw. I let him know what happened and that if it happened again, Anthony wouldn't be allowed back as a guest, even if that meant the entire firm blackballed us. Craig apologized and said he'd take care of it."

"Did you recognize the women he met?"

"No, but they were dressed sharp. Intimidating is what came to mind. And intelligent. And they looked like they'd had enough of Anthony Dunnegan. They didn't even stay for dinner. They told him what they had to say and then left. I don't think they were there for more than half an hour. Then he was *really* pissed. Tossed a twenty down on the table, which didn't even cover half of their drink tab or the appetizer he ordered, and got up. He knocked his chair over and his face was beet-red. Like I said, he was mad."

"I hope I never meet this man," Aunt Scarlet said. "I might have to use my shoes on him."

Richard looked confused by that announcement, but that's only because he didn't know that a click of her heels under the table might stab him in the foot.

"We kept an eye on Dunnegan," Richard continued. "He went into the bar and sulked for a little while. I had Brad add what he didn't cover at the table to his bar tab. And I added a gratuity for the poor girl he made cry."

"That's good thinking," Scarlet said. "I like you."

"Thank you, Ma'am."

"How long did Dunnegan stay at the bar?" I asked.

"That, I don't know. It was a Friday night dinner rush, so I got busy. By the time I had a chance to look up it was eleven o'clock and he was gone. But I knew Brad would've come to get me if things had gotten rough."

"I don't supposed Brad is available to talk?"

"Sure. I'll grab him for you and cover the bar a few minutes. We're ready to open for lunch. It was nice to have met you," Richard said to me and Scarlet. "And Mo, lunch is on the house today. It's good to see you."

"Good to see you too, my friend." They shook hands again and Richard headed toward the bar to get Brad.

"How do you know him so well?" I asked Mo.

Mo grinned and ate the last corn muffin. "That's Ugly Mo business right there, girl. Why don't you come work for me? I pay a lot more than you're making now."

I pressed my lips together and shook my head. "That's probably not a good idea. I'm thinking about getting engaged to a cop. The high chance of me going to prison might look bad for him. And I look terrible in orange."

"You're thinking about getting engaged to a *cop*?" Mo said incredulously. "Why you want to go and do that for?"

"You're back to your ghetto talk," I said.

"That's my native tongue," he said. "Marrying a cop is a horrible idea. It'll never last. Cops always have three or four wives. This guy divorced?"

I sat up very straight in my chair and twisted my napkin in my lap. "He was only married for a few months. It shouldn't even count as a marriage," I said primly, but there was a gnawing feeling in my stomach. And it wasn't because of the donuts.

"Uh huh," Mo said. "So you'll be number two. And you can bet there will be a number three and four. They work horrible hours and are addicted to the rush. That's no kind of life for a nice young lady like yourself."

"I don't know about all that cop stuff he's talking about," Scarlet butted in, "but I don't think you should do it because marriage is horrible. Why would you want to get married? You're single and free. Marriage just intensifies people's bad habits until you want to murder them in their sleep."

"If marriage is so horrible then why did you get married five times?" I asked, irritated with both of them now.

"Because I'm a romantic at heart," she said immediately. "Except you can't get too attached because sometimes they die. That's especially true if you marry a cop."

Fortunately, Brad walked up about that time and I was saved from having to think about that statement too much. I worried about Nick every day. Just like I'd worried about my dad every day. It wasn't always an easy job to love someone who loved to serve and protect. But they deserved to love people who could stick with them through it all.

Brad was rail-thin and had dark hair that he'd slicked back into a ponytail at the nape of his neck. He had a full mountain man beard and wore black-framed glasses. I think he was a hipster. He wore black slacks, a pressed white shirt, and a bowtie like the other employees, but he also wore a pair of black suspenders. I figured he only got away with it because he was the bartender.

"Mr. Drake said you guys wanted to talk to me," he said, taking Richard's vacant seat.

The restaurant had opened and people were coming inside to be seated.

"My name is Addison Holmes," I said, giving him my business card. "I just need to ask you some questions about the Friday night last week that Anthony Dunnegan was sitting at the bar."

"Yeah, what an asshole," Brad said, pushing his glasses up with one finger. "Excuse my language."

"Relax, boy," Scarlet said. "Only boring people and nuns don't cuss. I'd toss priests into that lot, but I met Father Cameron when I went to Scotland one summer and that man knew more ways to use the Lord's name than anyone I've ever known. 'Course, he was using them when he was in bed with me, so maybe it was more of a repentance thing, now that I think about it."

"Is this for real?" Brad asked. "Are we on *Candid Camera*?"

"Unfortunately, no," I said. "Tell us what happened with Anthony that night."

"Not much to tell, really," Brad said with a shrug. "He sat on the barstool on the far right and ordered a gin and tonic. He'd already had two at the table and you could tell he just wanted to get drunk. He was mad about something, and a real dick to me and one of the other bartenders. Mr. Drake told me to keep an eye on Dunnegan and let him know if there was any trouble, so that's what I did."

"Dunnegan mentioned a woman who came in and sat next to him. Do you remember her?"

Brad laughed and pushed his glasses up to the bridge of his nose again. "Do I remember her?" he asked. "I'll never be able to forget her. She was something else. Everyone in the bar was staring at her, men and women both." He rubbed his hand down over the length of his beard in an oddly soothing motion. "It was pretty crowded in the bar, and the only empty barstool was next to Dunnegan, because every time someone tried to sit there he was so awful to them they got up and left. So she sat and ordered a martini.

"It looked like she was waiting for someone, and she kept checking her phone. I felt kind of sorry for her after a while. I mean, I'm talking about a seriously gorgeous woman. Who would stand up somebody like that?"

"A question for the ages," I said, thinking of my own experiences of being stood up. "Did Dunnegan try to talk to her?"

"It was the first time all night he was tongue-tied. We all were. She looked just like…"

"Let me guess," I said. "Wonder Woman."

"I would've loved to see her in nothing but her magic bracelets," Brad said.

"I did a photo shoot similar to that about seventy years ago," Scarlet said. "They called them pin-ups back then."

"Whew, I would've liked to have seen that," Mo said, winking at Scarlet.

"I'm happy to show you next time you visit." Scarlet batted her eyelashes flirtatiously and I was pretty sure they were holding hands under the table, because their chairs had somehow gotten closer together.

I coughed loudly and covered my mouth with my fist, yelling, "Stop it," amid the coughs. There could not be more nights between them. Scarlet was ninety years old, for cripe's sake. She was going to break a hip or something. I took a sip of water and apologized for the coughing fit.

"How long did she stay?" I asked.

"They both had a couple more drinks," Brad said, shrugging. "And I guess she got bored because she finally started talking to him. It wasn't too long after that they asked for the tab and left. He paid both tabs, but I figure it was only because he was trying to impress her. I offered to call a cab for them, but they said they were going to walk. I figured they might go to the park or something or try to catch their own cab. I didn't see where they went after that."

We finished our lunch and Mo left a generous tip in cash for our waiter, and then we headed back to the van. I noticed a couple of pedi-cabs parked along the sidewalk.

"Let's take a quick ride," I said. "Dunnegan and the mystery woman got in a pedi-cab after they left the restaurant. I want to retrace the route."

"I always wanted to be a detective," Mo said. "But I like money. And I like knocking some sense into people when I got to. We were created with that animalistic instinct to protect what's ours— family, possessions, land—and people nowadays don't know how to take a stand for the things they believe in. What they gonna do? Xbox their enemies to death?" he said, shaking his head in disbelief. "The way I see it, my life is reflective of how God intended. I do unto others and all that shit. I protect my family. And sometimes I'm like Jesus at the temple, flipping tables and busting caps in people's asses when they don't do what they're supposed to."

I didn't remember anything in the Bible about busting a cap in anyone's ass, but maybe Mo had a newer translation.

The two pedi-cab drivers saw us coming, and one of them pedaled away before we could get there. I couldn't say I blamed him. The other froze and stared at us like a deer in the headlights. He was Asian and small of stature, and I was pretty sure I could've bench-pressed him if I'd tried. I felt bad about even making him attempt to cart us around. But Scarlet had already settled herself in the middle of the back seat and Mo held out his hand to help me in next to her.

I winced apologetically at the driver and he finally found his words. "A hundred dollars," he said. "Half up front." He held out a hand and I was ready to get out again.

We didn't need to retrace Dunnegan's steps that badly. But Mo took out his money clip from the inside pocket of his suit coat and peeled off a fifty, and then Mo took his seat on the other side of Scarlet. The carriage sunk under his weight and I hunched down into the seat, and flipped the collar of my coat up for good measure.

"My name's Moji," the driver said. "Where are you going?"

"Can you take us to Charlie's?" I asked.

"They ain't open, lady. You need a drink this early, your best bet is to head over to the Walgreens."

"I've been there," I said. "We just need a ride down to Charlie's and back."

"Whatever, lady. It's your money." And then he stood up on the pedals and pushed down, slowly putting us in motion.

At the pace we were going, I could've run circles around the pedi-cab, but it gave me time to let all the information I'd collected scramble around in my brain. I bit my lip in indecision. I was going to need help on this. But there were consequences to every action. Before I could talk myself out of it, my cell phone was in my hand and I was dialing.

"Savage," he answered.

"So," I said. And then I let an awkward silence follow.

Agent Matt Savage worked out of the FBI Satellite office in Savannah, and our relationship was a complicated one. Several months ago, Kate had included me in Savage's investigation to recover stolen Russian gems that had been lifted from a dead courier.

To say that there had been instant sparks between us would've been an understatement. Savage was like forbidden fruit. He was a little bit mysterious, a whole lot dangerous, and he liked to break the rules. He was my high school fantasy come to life.

He had a strong Native American heritage with a little bit of something else thrown in, but when you got down to it, he looked like the love child of The Rock and Pocahontas. He was gorgeous. And his body should've been used for modeling Calvin Klein underwear instead of the ugly black suits that were FBI standard. It was a damn crime against humanity, in my opinion.

Savage constantly wreaked havoc with my

moral compass, but I'd never succumbed to the temptation. And there had most definitely been temptation. But having been on the receiving end of unfaithfulness, I could never do that to someone I loved. And despite the ups and downs, I loved Nick.

I wasn't afraid to admit that Savage was a teensy bit of the reason I'd told Nick I needed to think about the marriage proposal. There had really been two major reasons. The first was that we'd just come off a big case and it had most definitely been life or death. I wanted to make sure Nick wasn't proposing because of a knee-jerk reaction since I could've died. The second reason was Savage. Right as Nick was popping the question, down on bended knee no less, Savage knocked on the door and interrupted the moment. And Savage hadn't been one bit sorry.

I hadn't been happy with him, and had put distance between me and *both* of the testosterone-driven men in my life. That was, until last week, when I'd been tracking down the Romeo Bandit at a nudist colony. The Romeo Bandit had been on the FBI's Most Wanted list for a really long time, so I'd had no choice but to call Savage in. It hadn't helped that when he'd gotten there I'd been naked as a jaybird. It had made things…awkward. And I hadn't talked to him since.

"Addison?" he said."

"Oh right," I said, thunking my hand against my head. "I need a little assistance. If you're available." I could practically hear his smile on the other end of the line.

"Darling, I'm always available. You only have to ask."

"Not in that way," I hissed. "In a federal way."

"Who are you talking to?" Aunt Scarlet asked.

"Agent Savage," I answered. The cart was rolling at a snail's pace and I could tell Scarlet was getting impatient.

"He's a hottie," she said. "But I already crossed a Native American off my list."

"I'm sure he'll be devastated to hear it." Savage was laughing in my ear and I rolled my eyes.

"I might be free to offer some federal assistance," Savage said. "Did you give Nick an answer yet?"

"Whether or not you'll help me is based on if I'm getting married or not?" I asked. My palms were getting sweaty and I rubbed them on my jeans.

"Of course not. Just curious."

"Then no," I answered. "I still have a few days left." There was another awkward pause. "I cut my hair," I blurted out.

The brilliant idea came to me that I just needed to make myself seem undesirable to Savage. Savage wasn't relationship material. Savage was bump in the night kind of material. I mean, it would be a hell of a bump, but there wouldn't be anything to show for it afterwards.

"Okaaay," Savage said, drawing out the word.

"Never mind," I said. "I've got this case. A guy, who's a real ass by the way, walks into a bar, and a beautiful woman sits down next to him. They have some drinks and leave together. One moment he's a member of the mile-high pedi-cab club and the next he's waking up in a bathtub full of ice and missing his kidney."

"Like the urban legend?" Savage asked.

"Yep, just like that. Guy doesn't want to file a report with the police because he doesn't want his wife or the media to find out that he's a schmuck. So he comes to us. And then Kate does a little digging and we find a similar case over in Hilton

Head six months ago. Only that time they took the heart, so it was a homicide. Then I'm doing a little more digging and it was mentioned that several years ago the same thing happened to a woman up in Atlanta."

"What do you need from me?" Savage asked.

"For starters, can you get me information on the woman in Atlanta, specifically her blood type? The connection between the victims is that they all have a rare blood type."

"Making it difficult for people who need transplants to find donors," Savage finished.

"Exactly."

"What else do you need?"

"A nationwide search of like crimes. Just anything that pops. I can look through the details. You can get the information a lot faster than I can and we need to get this one wrapped up."

"Why? Because you've got a big question to answer?"

"Nooooo," I said, rolling my eyes. "Because if I don't wrap this up I'm going to end up doing bodily harm to the client."

"Have Scarlet take care of him," Savage said.

"She shot a man's ear off the other day."

"Well, there you go." Savage disconnected and I assumed that meant he was going to help me out.

CHAPTER THIRTEEN

CHARLIE'S WAS A little dive bar a few blocks away on the corner.

Moji had been right. There wasn't a soul in sight, and the bar was closed up tight. It said on the doors they didn't open again until four o'clock. I looked at my watch. Nothing could be done here for a couple more hours.

Something yellow caught the corner of my eye and jogged my memory about the conversation I'd had with Anthony Dunnegan. He'd mentioned he and the mystery woman had ridden in a yellow pedi-cab. It was going to be like finding a needle in a haystack, but if I could find that pedi-cab driver, he might be able to tell us something more about the mystery woman. Maybe he even helped her if she made it seemed like Dunnegan had passed out. Or maybe he overheard a phone conversation.

I'd phone the cab company later and see what

kind of records they kept. Probably not good ones, if I had to guess by looking at the ragtag group of pedi-cab drivers. Male or female, all of the ones lined up on the street had an unwashed hippie vibe going for them. They all had varying levels of dreadlocks. Many of them wore long shorts despite the low temperatures, and long-sleeved tees. Tattoos peeked from beneath their clothing and they spoke in a fast-paced code that included a lot of waving hands and knuckle bumps.

The dude in the yellow pedi-cab wasn't fairing as well as the others. He was asleep in the back of his cab, his long yellow dreads hanging across his face.

"There's a dead man in that cab," Scarlet said, pointing. "I'm surprised no one has stolen his hair."

I looked at her confused. "What in the world would they want his hair for?"

"People steal every damned thing nowadays," she said. "When I lived in France someone stole my neighbor's front lawn. Weirdest thing I ever saw. They pulled up all the sod, every plant, and even the garden gnomes. Nothing but dirt left when they were through."

"Hell, that's nothing," Mo said. "I know a guy that had all the gold teeth taken right out of his mouth. Never even knew it. Just woke up looking like a jack-o-lantern."

"He's not dead," Moji said, looking over his shoulder at us. "That's Raf. He doesn't really wake up until sometime after three. He says it's not worth peddling sober people around all day. They don't tip and always want to ask questions."

"He sleeps in his cab?" I asked.

"Just some of the time. He gets up early and parks out here with the others first thing in the morning so he can get in the lineup, and then he goes back to sleep until he's ready for his shift."

My phone rang and I didn't recognize the number, but it was a Savannah area code so I answered.

"Addison Holmes," I said.

"You want to tell me why you're in a pedi-cab with Ugly Mo and Aunt Scarlet? I can't imagine why you thought it'd be a good idea to continue your association with him."

"Hey, I'm a grown woman," I said. "I can make my own decisions."

"Damn straight, you can," Scarlet said. "Who

are you talking to now?"

"It's Nick," I whispered.

"Is Nick the one you're thinking of marrying?" she asked.

"Shh," I said, putting my finger over my lips. "How did you know I was here?" I asked.

"There are eyes all over this city. People are always watching."

I scanned the streets until I came across Bryan Diamond. He was working mounted patrol and looked miserable. I'd met Bryan last year at the department's Christmas party when he'd been a captain. Sometime between then and New Year's Eve he'd been demoted to sergeant and assigned six months on mounted patrol. I had no idea what he'd done to earn the slap down, but it must've been really bad.

He noticed that I'd spotted him, and I glared in his direction. He just grinned and pulled at the reins to send his horse in the opposite direction. I guess he had to find his entertainment where he could.

"Tell Diamond he'd better pray I don't get a hold of him."

"I'm sure that'll terrify him," Nick said. "I believe he was at the station that time you jumped on the desk because a mouse ran across your foot."

"That's different," I said defensively. "And maybe I won't have to touch Bryan. Maybe his horse will get a bad case of diarrhea while Bryan is out on patrol. I'm sure people would get a real kick out of watching Bryan sitting on a horse that's shitting all over Savannah."

"Such language, Addison," Scarlet said. "But I'm liking the way your mind is working. You're a Holmes, through and through."

Nick paused on the other end of the line. "Jesus," he said. "That's terrifying. And to think I still want to marry you. I must be a glutton for punishment."

Nick disconnected and I was feeling oddly upbeat. I'm not sure if it was because I liked the idea of getting revenge on Bryan or because Nick still wanted to marry me.

Moji dropped us back at the van and he was shaking so hard he could barely clasp the other fifty-dollar bill Mo held out to him. I figured he was smart to ask for the hundred dollars. There was no way he'd have the energy to peddle anyone else today—maybe not tomorrow either—and he probably made twice what he does on a normal night.

We got in the van and I debated whether or not to tell Ugly Mo about my run-in with Fat Louie's man. I finally decided I had enough on my plate without having the added stress of Big Eddie trying to "fuck me up." Not to mention, word was obviously out about what Scarlet did to Javier's ear.

"So I have a little problem with the van," I told Mo.

"Girl, I got a no-return policy. Even if you are entertaining for Ugly Mo. I'm going to line item you for my accountant."

"I appreciate that," I said. "But the problem is I met a friend of Fat Louie's over at the Tiger Lounge the other night while I was waiting for Jasmine to leave for the night. I put a gun in his face, so he's not too happy with me. And it's a slight possibility that the guy whose ear Scarlet shot off was also an employee of Fat Louie."

I told him what happened with the van being spray-painted and taking it over to Magic Mike's to be repaired.

"That's damned disrespectful," Mo said, shaking his head. "There's no honor in the business anymore. Louie is a disgrace. An embarrassment. His mother was the brains behind his whole organization and he up and killed her. Now he's just a monster running loose in my city. I can't have that anymore. And if Jasmine is tied up with him, then I'll take her down with him."

Mo stamped his cane against the floor of the van in indignation and I jumped at the sound. I dropped them both off at The Ballastone, so Scarlet could take her afternoon nap and Mo could rearrange some faces. At least that's what he'd told me he was going to do when he said goodbye.

I had to admit, I'd become rather fond of Ugly Mo. He wasn't a half bad guy, if you overlooked all the crimes he was committing. And I hadn't heard anyone say that he was a murderer like Fat Louie, so maybe he wasn't one of the really bad criminals. Though I should probably keep that opinion to myself. I was pretty sure Nick wouldn't agree.

CHAPTER FOURTEEN

I WASN'T AS lucky finding a parking spot going back to the agency. At least not a spot that didn't require me to work parallel parking magic that I didn't possess. Instead, I parked six blocks away down a street where one of the buildings was under construction. I assumed there were no cars parked on the street just in case a piece of construction equipment rammed into their car. I was oddly okay with it.

The walk back to the agency didn't take long, and when I walked up the stairs and into the foyer I immediately smelled chocolate chip cookies. Lucy was sitting at her desk, her long red nails clacking at the keyboard.

"Who has the cookies?" I asked, closing the door behind me.

Lucy ignored me and went about her typing. Her desk was a big mahogany behemoth that was shaped like a U. I approached the desk and decided to try another approach. "Anything come in for me?"

She kept typing with her right hand and picked up one of the loose notes she kept organized ruthlessly on her desk, and handed it to me.

"Did you hear me about the cookies?" I asked again, but it was of no use. Every tactic I'd ever tried failed. I'd never once heard Lucy say a single word. "They smell good. And I really need one."

She stopped her clacking on the keyboard and I thought I'd finally gotten through the barrier. Instead she pointed her finger in the direction of the conference room and then went back to typing.

"Someday," I said with sigh, "I'm going to get you to spill your secrets. You won't know what hit you."

I unbuttoned my coat and headed straight for the conference room instead of my office. I was pulling apart the Velcro to take the holster from around my waist when I pushed open the door and came face to face with Savage.

"Need help with that?" he asked, eyeing my midriff.

I froze and stared for a few seconds. He was dressed for work in his habitual black suit and white shirt, but he'd left his tie off and the first couple of buttons of his collar were undone.

"I wasn't expecting to see you here."

"Sure you were. You can't dangle a case like this in front of me and not expect me to bite."

I felt my insides do a slow roll when he said the word bite. That conjured images I wasn't altogether comfortable with.

"Stop it," I said, narrowing my eyes and getting my hormones under control.

He held up his hands in surrender. "I'm not doing anything." He grinned and I knew as well as he did that he was full of baloney. "I brought cookies."

"I should've known it was you," I said, eyeing the box of cookies on the table. I could tell they were still warm and gooey.

Kate chose that moment to join us and she headed straight for the cookie box, not making polite conversation until she'd bitten into one and felt the sugar rush through her bloodstream.

"I'm glad you called in Savage," Kate said, taking a chair. "I figure we're working this thing wrong. We need to work it in micro levels, like a crime scene. You're focused on Anthony Dunnegan. But he's alive."

"Unfortunately," I said, making Savage snort with laughter. It was then I noticed Kate had the magnetic whiteboards out.

"We know there are several like crimes that have been committed over the last several years, but they're in different cities and states. Working little pieces of a lot of cases isn't going to help us solve this case. At least not to the satisfaction of our client. What we need to do is focus on the crime that happened last week. We need to treat it as if it is an active murder investigation, so that's what you're going to do," Kate said, looking at me. "And Savage and I are going to try to see what we can pull together on the other victims. If we're lucky, we can tie it all up in a big red bow."

"You'd better let Addison eat a cookie before you get too deep into this," Savage said. "She's got that look."

I didn't have to be told twice. I headed to the table and grabbed a warm cookie. And then I grabbed another for good measure and took a seat. Kate could be long-winded in these kinds of meetings.

Kate was great at this part of the job, and I often wondered how she'd been able to give up police work. Sometimes I wondered if something had happened she'd never told me about. Because she really seemed to love it.

She set up the boards with pictures. The first had Jonathon Hunt, Anthony Dunnegan, and a woman I didn't recognize on it.

"That's Abby Rhodes," Kate said before I could ask. "Our Atlanta victim with the missing heart." Then she put up six other photographs beneath the three on top and my eyes widened. "And these are the hits that came up in just the short amount of time since you called Savage. Nine victims, ranging in age from twenty to forty-seven. All with type O-negative blood. All but two of them were killed, and all in a six-state radius— Florida, Georgia, North and South Carolina, Tennessee, and Alabama."

Savage read off data to her while I watched and ate cookies. The pedi-cab ride had given me an appetite. Beneath each picture, Kate wrote what state the victims were found in and what organ was taken from them. On the middle board she posted what hotel each victim was found in. There were no repeats, or even the same chain used.

"Work it out hypothetically," Savage said. "We're running a black market organ donor ring. Who do we need in place to make it work successfully?"

"I'd say the biggest part of the job is someone who can do the surgery," I said. "The medical examiner's report on Hunt and the hospital report on Dunnegan both said the same thing. The surgery was done by a professional, in their opinion, as it was done so well."

On the third board Kate wrote *surgeon* at the top.

"The surgeon isn't the mastermind. The surgeon is a necessary tool for a successful operation," Savage said. "Money is always the motive for something like this."

"Ugly Mo said prices started around two hundred and fifty thousand dollars," I said.

"*Ugly Mo*?" Savage asked, shaking with silent laughter. "You're friends with Ugly Mo Jackson? I'm sure Nick is loving that."

"We're not friends," I said. "I mean, we're kind of friendly. I think he and Aunt Scarlet had sex, but I don't want to think about that if I don't have to."

"Christ, that's a horrible image," Kate said with a grimace.

"You'll be glad to know she explained to me why Mo needs the cane to walk with."

Kate and Savage both broke down with laughter.

"If I were them, I'd be shopping for clients, right?" I said. "There's a national transplant list. The people on the list have to be ready to go at a moment's notice, as soon as the organ becomes available. It's a very time-sensitive process."

"Okay, so a *transporter*," Kate said, listing it under surgeon. "Which means they're doing both surgeries not too far away from each other."

"There's no way the donor could receive the organ in a hotel room," I said. "The recovery period is too long. They'd need equipment and they'd need to stay close by the patient for at least a little while to make sure that nothing went wrong. When you're paying that much money for your life, you're going to want some kind of guarantee that it's going to work. If they couldn't do the surgery in a hotel or a hospital, really, the only thing left is the recipient's home."

"It's only been a little over a week since Dunnegan's kidney was taken," Kate said. "They might still be in the area."

"The surgeon wouldn't take care of the patient on a day-to-day basis," Savage said.

"But a nurse would," Kate and I said at the same time, and she added *nurse* to the board.

"That would also provide an explanation for all the medications they would need for just one surgery. Anesthesia for the victim and the organ recipient. Then all the drugs to help the recipient adjust to the new organ."

"Why not just write a prescription and let the pharmacy take care of it?" I asked. "A lot easier to do that than try to steal the right amounts from a hospital without getting caught."

"And that's not something we could check because of privacy laws," Savage said. "They could be filling prescriptions right down the street and we'd never have a clue."

"You mentioned a shopping list," Kate said. "That the financers would be shopping for clients who not only fit the income bracket, but also the rare blood type they need to drive the price up.

Who has access to the transplant list?"

"That's easy enough to check on," Savage said, making a few notes and then opening his laptop.

I looked at my watch and saw it was almost four o'clock. I needed to get back in action so I could talk to someone at Charlie's before things got too crazy. And then I needed to hit the Comfort Inn where Anthony Dunnegan's surgery was done and talk to the night manager.

"I need to get back out there," I said. "Seeing the big picture like this really helped reorganize things in my mind. I'll keep y'all posted. I'm going to use Rosemarie for backup tonight if she's available. Sometimes things don't go as planned when we work together, so I may need you both on call."

Kate and Savage both stared at me with identical expressions, and I waved my fingers at them and left. Then I came back inside and grabbed a few more cookies for the road. Rosemarie would be upset if I didn't bring her any.

CHAPTER FIFTEEN

S CHOOL WAS OUT for the afternoon, so Rosemarie answered her phone on the first ring.

"I was hoping you would call," she said. "Guess who's back in town?"

I could hear her nervous giddiness at being the first to be able to tell me the news. My mother had tried to call three times yesterday. I'd let all of them go to voicemail for a couple of reasons. The first being that she always called on Sundays to check to see if I'd be attending services, just in case she needed to save me a seat in the pew. The second reason being that I wanted to avoid any conversation that might include Aunt Scarlet. My mother and Scarlet got along like oil and water. Probably because they were so much alike.

But there was also the possibility that she'd been wanting to pass on whatever news it was that

Rosemarie was about to tell me. There wasn't a lot to do in Whiskey Bayou, so gossip was a big pastime. And my mother always prided herself on having the most up to date information. She was better than TMZ.

"Who?" I asked, not really caring. People didn't really leave Whiskey Bayou. It was like a black hole. You might try to escape, but familial roots would suck you back in eventually.

"Veronica Wade. She came driving through town, proud as punch in a little white BMW yesterday. Even had the top down to make sure everyone saw her passing through. Had a man with her in the passenger seat. Poor fellow."

I'd headed back to my office to change clothes. I couldn't exactly go out to a bar and hope to get any information dressed in yoga pants and a sweatshirt, but Rosemarie's news stopped me cold.

Veronica Wade was my archenemy. I *loathed* her. And it wasn't just because she was the one my fiancé had decided to consummate our non-marriage with. We'd gone through school together and she'd been a terror. She was worse as an adult, and I hadn't been able to escape her, because we'd taught together at James Madison High as well.

"She was visiting her mother," Rosemarie went on. "I've heard Delores is in a real bad way after the scandal with you and Veronica last year. Apparently she's become a recluse and a hoarder, and now she's bedridden because her heart can't take the strain. Doctor Chance's wife told my mother that they were expecting her to keel over at any moment. I guess Veronica was just paying her last respects."

I grunted noncommittally. I didn't have anything nice to say, so I figured it was best to keep my mouth shut. I closed my office door behind me and put Rosemarie on speaker so I could change clothes.

"And Carol Labo saw her at the gas station and told me that Veronica got her implants fixed and they were bigger than ever, and that she got a new nose job. You know there's bad blood between Carol and Veronica, so Carol said she just smiled sweetly and asked Veronica if they meant to put her new nose on crooked like that. Stunned Veronica speechless long enough that Carol was able to drive away without Veronica clawing her eyes out. I would've like to have seen it myself."

"Veronica's all in the past," I said, pulling on a

pair of leggings and a little black skirt. "What she does is no concern of mine any longer. I don't have to see her little beady eyes staring at me from down the hall anymore, so I consider that a win. She's a miserable and unhappy woman who finds pleasure in trying to destroy others. She'll reap what she sows one day."

"That's a very adult way of looking at it," Rosemarie said, surprise evident in her voice.

"Thank you. Besides, I heard from my mother who heard from one of the ladies that works in the gynecologist's office that Veronica contracted a really stubborn case of the clap. I figure that's just karma being a bitch."

I didn't have a huge variety of clothes in my suitcase, but I found a long-sleeved, stretchy, black wrap shirt that made my cleavage look good, and I found a silver necklace with a dangly pendant that hung between my breasts to break up all the black.

"I need some backup tonight," I told her. "You in?"

There was silence on the other end for a few seconds and then I heard Rosemarie's excited exhalation of air. "You bet. I'm heading that way now. Give me fifteen minutes."

"Take thirty. You're going to want to come dressed for a night out."

"Like a superhero?" she asked.

"No, like a normal person going out for the evening," I said. "We don't want to attract too much attention."

"Got it. Incognito," she said.

I sighed and pulled out the black high-heeled booties with the silver buckles and slid my feet inside them. Incognito could mean any number of things to Rosemarie.

"Oh, by the way," I said. "Tell Magic Mike thanks for the paint job. I didn't expect him to not charge me."

"You were right about letting him be on the bottom. Didn't have to worry about his lack of rhythm at all. Of course, he hurt his back toward the end there. I told him I had things under control, but you know how men are. They don't listen worth squat."

I just agreed to keep her from going into any more detail. We decided Rosemarie would park at the agency in half an hour and we'd leave from there in the van. Oddly enough, I still felt com-forted by Ugly Mo's assurance that he was going to take care of things with Fat Louie.

I was feeling pretty good, despite the continued stiffness down the left side of my body from my fall, but the Icy Hot had helped tremendously and I could mostly move without groaning. I slicked on some sassy red lipstick and added some silver dangle earrings that matched the pendant.

I still had twenty minutes until Rosemarie arrived, so I decided to call the pedi-cab companies and see if there was a way to find out who'd been working the area outside of Charlie's on the Friday night Anthony lost his kidney.

I did an internet search and came up with two different pedi-cab companies that served the Savannah area. I was dialing the first number when I noticed something glaringly obvious.

Tri-Star Pedi-Cabs served the downtown Savannah area, and their cabs were red with the Tri-Star logo on the back along with their phone number. Moji had been an employee of Tri-Star. The other company was called Garden City Pedi-Cabs and their cabs were a dark hunter-green with gold writing on the back. From what I could tell, there were no other companies listed. Which begged the question, who was the dreadlocked guy in the yellow pedi-cab and what company did he belong to?

It was still ten minutes until Rosemarie arrived, and I was starting to get antsy. The pedi-cab angle was really niggling at me, and I could've kicked myself for not trying to talk to the dreadlocked driver when I'd see him earlier in the day.

I grabbed my red Kate Spade clutch and shoved my lipstick, keys, money, and ID inside, and then headed toward the front lobby. It was almost five o'clock and it was starting to get dark outside. Lucy was away from her desk and the halls were quiet. I was assuming that Kate and Savage were still working the other angles and that they'd call if anything new came up.

My cellphone rang just as I reached the door and I saw it was Aunt Scarlet.

"Addison," she whispered. "You've got to rescue me. Get me out of here."

"What happened? Are you okay? Give me an address and I'm on my way."

"I'm calling from the bathroom at The Ballastone. I've changed my mind. I *do* want to go back. I can't take it anymore. I'm ninety years old, even though I've been told I could pass for sixty-five, but I'm just plum worn out."

I was trying to grasp what she was talking about. And then it hit me. Mo had told her once she went black, she'd never go back. I stopped and thumped my head against the wall.

"I found out he takes those little blue pills. What the heck does he expect me to do with that sucker for four hours? I can't feel my lady parts anymore. They're completely numb. I don't think I'm meant for an anaconda. I'm good with a plain old boa constrictor any day of the week. Or maybe I need to switch to garden snakes, but I hate to set my sights so low."

"Please, Lord," I said while my head was still pressed against the wall. "If you have any mercy at all, just strike me dead."

"I told Mo he'd have to use that pill on somebody else tonight, because I've got to go out with you. He said he appreciated my work ethic and that maybe his wife was home. So can you come get me? He's waiting here to make sure I get out okay. I think he's worried about me, which is sweet, but annoying. I was so tuckered out after the last go around that I passed out for a little while. I think he thought he'd killed me."

"I'll come get you right now," I said, just to get her to stop talking. "Meet me out front."

I sent Rosemarie a text and let her know I had to run a quick errand and that I'd be back in a few minutes, and then I ran outside and remembered I'd had to park six blocks away.

"Dammit," I said. I was in heels and in a hurry.

My phone buzzed again and I looked down to see the Nick alarm. A black muscle truck slid to a stop in front of me and the passenger side window rolled down.

"Need a ride?" Nick asked.

"Actually, I do, if you don't mind." I hitched myself into the truck and told him where I'd parked. "I'm kind of in a hurry."

Nick gritted his teeth and smiled, and I could tell he was still annoyed with me about the Ugly Mo thing.

"I'm going to assume you're heading out to work," he said. "I can't imagine where you've got your gun hidden in that outfit."

I pinched my lips tight and said, "Wouldn't you like to know." But I wanted to roll my eyes. I'd been in such a hurry that I'd forgotten to put it back on after I'd changed.

"Because I know you wouldn't be dumb enough to be traipsing around unarmed after you and Ugly Mo have become such good friends."

I sat up very straight in the seat. "Of course I'm armed," I lied. "And Mo is actually a very nice man. As far as I can tell," I said as an afterthought. "I think he and Aunt Scarlet are kind of dating."

The little vein in Nick's temple throbbed. "He's a criminal. He brokers every illegal deal in the Southeast United States."

"He told me he was a broker," I said primly. "But it's not like I'm hanging out with him on purpose. All I did was buy a car from the man. I wasn't expecting Scarlet to seduce him and bring him along for the ride. None of this is my fault."

Nick grimaced and turned onto the street where the van was parked. It didn't look like it had been damaged and there were no new messages spray-painted along the sides.

"It's never your fault," he said. "But you somehow always end up right in the middle of things. I'm hearing whispers that Kate put you on the Anthony Dunnegan case. I asked around. George Carmichel was the officer who responded when the ambulance brought Anthony to the hospital. The department really tried to put pressure on Dunnegan to file a report, but he wouldn't do it. He was scared shitless."

"Considering he'd just had his kidney surgically removed, I'm not all that surprised."

"Something as well-orchestrated as the Anthony Dunnegan job wasn't done by amateurs. It's a network that would need constantly moving parts and contacts. Do you know who facilitates those kinds of jobs?" Nick asked.

I was getting a sinking feeling in my stomach, but didn't say anything.

"A *broker* does," he continued. "It's funny your acquaintance with Ugly Mo started at the same time you picked up this case."

I wasn't totally convinced, but Nick had planted seeds of doubt in my mind. Mo had admitted to having knowledge about the organization. Maybe he was more involved than he'd let on.

"My point is," Nick said. "I love you. I want you safe. And when I see you in potential danger I just want to protect you. Can you understand that?"

He'd taken the edge right off my anger. "Yes,"

I told him softly. I felt the same way when he went to work every day.

"Good."

He grabbed me by the back of the neck and pulled me toward him, kissing me long and hard, until I was breathless and couldn't quite remember why I'd been in such a hurry to begin with. And then I did remember. Scarlet was with Ugly Mo. And she could be in more danger than she thought.

"I've got to go," I said, pushing open the truck door.

"Be safe. And call me if you need anything. Don't be stubborn because your deadline is ticking."

"You just had to throw that in there, didn't you?" I asked.

Nick grinned and I felt my heart flip slowly in my chest. I waved bye and hopped in the van. The good news about parking six blocks from the agency was that I was closer to The Ballastone. I peeled out into the street in my haste. I didn't breathe a sigh of relief until I saw Scarlet standing at the base of the stairs next to the bellman. Ugly Mo was nowhere in sight, and I felt myself relax.

And then I saw the horrified look on the bell-man's face and realized the reason. Scarlet was wearing black leggings, a black long-sleeved shirt, and a white, rabbit fur vest. She had on knee-high riding boots and a black-and-white silk scarf tied artfully around her perfectly coifed hair. She looked like a perfectly respectable grandmotherly type, in the style of Jackie Onassis. The only problem was that she had a giant bag of ice between her legs that came up the front and back like a sanitary napkin and she had it fastened to her body with black duct tape. It looked like she was wearing an ice diaper.

My eyes met the bellman's, and I could tell he was going to need a lot of therapy to recover, but he opened the passenger side door for Scarlet and held her arms as she got settled in.

"Umm," I said once we pulled away from the hotel and were headed back to pick up Rosemarie.

"Ingenious, isn't it?" she asked. "I figured it'd at least help the swelling go down. It reminds me of back in the war days when all I had was my wits and the materials at hand. I once made a catapult out of branches, my undergarments, and rosary beads. I sent a coded message right into the general's bedroom. Saved a lot of lives with that one."

I pressed my lips together and circled around Telfair Square so we'd pull up directly in front of the agency. I spotted Rosemarie from the other end of the block.

The word incognito must have multiple definitions. She was wearing a long-sleeved, canary-yellow, one-piece jumpsuit and black wedge heels. I couldn't decide if she looked more like the guys that collect hazardous waste or a Teletubby, but whichever it was, incognito she was not. Her hair was back to its Farrah Fawcett glory and she was wearing fake eyelashes that looked a little like spiders.

"What's that up there?" Scarlet asked, squinting. "Looks like Big Bird with a camel toe. You think we could get a drink somewhere? My baby-maker burns like fire, and this ice is so cold I can't tell if it's doing the job or I've wet myself."

I stopped the van next to Rosemarie, and she climbed in the back. I wasn't surprised by Rosemarie's attire. Somewhere deep inside, I'd known "nighttime party" Rosemarie was going to show up. And I couldn't say I was all that surprised by Scarlet's ice diaper. It was always something. All in all, it was a normal Monday night out.

CHAPTER SIXTEEN

I CIRCLED AROUND the block a couple of times, not only looking for a good parking place, but also looking for the yellow pedi-cab. I guess Raf had found some clients that were drunk enough to transport, because he was in the wind.

The good news was, Scarlet had decided her lady parts were feeling better and she was going to leave the ice bag in the sink in the back of the van.

Charlie's wasn't crowded, which was to be expected on a Monday night before six, so we walked through the front doors and immediately became the object of everyone's attention. We were certainly eye-catching.

We found spots at the bar and the bartender lifted her brows at us as she filled an order. I was trying to size her up before I decided which approach I was going to take. She came closer to take our orders and I noticed the crease around her left ring finger where a wedding ring had once been.

"What can I get y'all?" she asked.

She was wearing jeans and a plaid shirt and her dark blonde hair was pulled into a messy bun on top of her head. Both of her ears had piercings all the way up and she had a tiny diamond stud in her nose. She was maybe thirty, and she seemed to be at peace with her profession of choice.

Rosemarie ordered a Sex on the Beach, Scarlet ordered a martini dry with two olives, and I ordered a glass of white wine.

"Can I ask you a question," I said to the bartender. I smiled, but I needed her to see the vulnerability lurking behind the smile.

"Sure thing, honey. What's up?"

I pulled out a picture of Anthony Dunnegan and slid it across the bar to her. "Do you happen to remember if this man came in here with another woman?"

I bit my lip and tried to work up some tears, but I wasn't that good of an actor. Thankfully, Rosemarie and Scarlet stayed silent.

"It's okay if he was with another woman," I said. "I can take it. I've known it all along, but I just need the proof to give to my attorney for the divorce."

"I hear ya," she said. "I hope you take him to the cleaners." She studied the photograph closely. "I don't know, honey. A lot of men come in this bar. When was he here?"

"Friday before last. A couple of reliable sources said he was with a woman who looked like…well, it sounds silly. But they said she looked like Wonder Woman. The new one," I said, clarifying before she could ask.

"Now that *does* sound familiar. Hold on a sec and let me get your drinks. I think Sheila might have been waiting on them. Your husband is kind of forgettable, and if I remember right he was a real ass, but the woman stood out. My name is Gina, by the way."

She made our drinks and then made a come here gesture to someone behind us. A few minutes later another woman appeared. She was older than Gina by probably a decade and a little broader in the hip. She wore a denim skirt and a tight rhinestone t-shirt, and her dark hair was long and straight. Age lines were prominent around her eyes and mouth. My mother would've said she looked like she'd been ridden hard and put away wet.

"Sheila, didn't you serve this guy Friday before last?" Gina asked her. "My friend here is about to skin him in a divorce for cheating on her."

"Hmmph," Sheila said. "They're all cheaters. Not worth the time or trouble."

"That's the truth," Scarlet said. "My third husband cheated on me once. I took my fillet knife and held it right against his penis. Gave him a real nice haircut and only nicked him a couple times. He didn't cheat on me again. Course, he died a couple weeks later." She paused for dramatic effect and then added, "Of natural causes." And then she finished off her martini.

"Christ," Sheila said. "That's hardcore."

"That's how I roll," Scarlet said.

"Damn right," Rosemarie said, and she and Scarlet toasted each other.

Sheila stared at the photograph for a couple of seconds and said, "Yeah, I remember that guy. He came in with Stella."

I perked up at that. "Oh no. Is she a friend of yours?" I asked, sounding discouraged. "Damn, I really wanted to get that cheating bastard." I was really getting into it.

"Not a personal friend, but she's been in a few times over the past few weeks. A couple times she just sat by herself and kind of watched everyone. Didn't respond to any guys trying to pick her up. And a couple times she came in with a few girl-friends. I figured maybe she was gay and didn't want the hassle. We never talked or anything, but I ran her credit card a few times. The name on it was Stella, but I don't remember the last name. Something Italian, I think. But then she came in with this douche a week or so ago."

Gina elbowed her friend. "That's her hus-band," she said, nodding to me.

"Oh right. Sorry about that," Sheila said.

"No problem. I think he's a douche too. It's better to know than to be duped and keep believ-ing his lies."

Then Sheila went into a play-by-play of how despicably Anthony acted with this Stella woman. They were both drinking, but Anthony was really throwing them back. She said Stella was a little more reserved, but she seemed pretty blitzed too. "I remember Jack had to ask them to leave, because things were getting pretty risqué out of the dance floor."

"Who's Jack?" I asked.

"Our bouncer," Gina answered.

"Yeah, Jack said your husband was really pissed off and started spouting off about lawsuits and stuff like that, but the woman just laughed and dragged him out of the bar. I don't know where they went from there."

"I really appreciate y'all's help," I told them gratefully. "Every piece of the puzzle I can put together is another nail in his coffin."

They both wished me well and Scarlet paid the tab, tipping them generously. I noticed Scarlet was walking funny on the way out and felt guilty for not parking closer after her traumatic afternoon with the anaconda.

"Would you mind pulling the van around?" I asked Rosemarie. "I'm not sure Scarlet's up to making the walk back. I'll stay here with her so she's not alone."

"You know, I didn't take it into consideration before," Scarlet said, "But you don't think Ugly Mo could get me pregnant, do you? I've been off birth control a lot of years, but it seems Mo might be more potent than most, considering that he can really get up in those hard to reach places."

"I wouldn't worry too much," I told her. "Probably Mo isn't potent enough to reverse menopause."

"That's a relief. I'd be a hundred and eight by the time that kid graduated from high school. I've got a lot of good years left."

I gave Rosemarie the car keys and she headed around the corner toward the van. Coming around the other corner at the same time was the yellow pedi-cab. In the driver's seat was Raf with the dreadlocks, only he was awake now.

"Shit," I said. "I really need to talk to that guy."

"Well, let's go then," Scarlet said. "At least I'll be sitting down. Rosemarie will probably be another ten minutes."

I weighed my options and decided it wasn't worth losing him to another customer or having him disappear the rest of the night, so I grabbed Scarlet by the arm and we headed across the street, waving our arms to flag him down.

"Hey there, could we get a ride?" I asked. "She had a little too much to drink."

"And I got swollen lady parts on account I did the deed with my first black man today."

"Righteous," Raf said. "I hear you'll never go back."

Seeing Raf awake wasn't much different than seeing him asleep. He had that vacant, zoned-out look of someone who'd taken one too many hits from his bong. He wore a pair of cargo shorts and a sweatshirt that said *Just Say No to Condoms.*

"Where y'all headed?"

"Over to the Hamilton Inn," I said, thinking I could kill two birds with one trip.

"Lame. There's no party there. It's got no vibe, man."

"I think she's had all the vibe she can handle for the day," I told him.

"Bummer." He started peddling and we coasted up Broughton Street at a much faster pace than we had on our trip earlier in the day. I sent a quick text to Rosemarie and told her to meet us over at the Hamilton Inn.

"We saw you earlier today," Scarlet said. "But you were sleeping. You looked real comfortable."

"Yeah, man. Like, this business isn't worth getting out of bed before three. Daytime people are a real drag."

"I was impressed that no one stole your hair,"

she said, as if that were a normal thing.

"I was worried about that at first," Raf said. " 'Cause it took me a while to grow my hair this way. I'm like, envied among my peers. It's like back when everyone was stealing all the Air Jordan's right off people's feet."

"Dark times," Scarlet said.

"The darkest," he agreed. "But I'm protected, man. I got nothing to worry about."

"How are you protected?" I asked.

He turned in his bicycle seat and stared at me like I was the one with the drug problem. "Umm, *God* protects me. He bought me this cart and the bicycle and he said I will protect you. So I was like, awesome. And then we smoked a joint."

"You smoked a joint with God?"

"Fuckin' A," he said.

"Is that why your cart is yellow and all the others in the city are red and green?" I asked.

He stopped for a light and beeped his little bicycle horn at another pedi-cab coming in our direction.

"No, man. I'm yellow because yellow is the color of good energy. I represent freedom and the fucking spirit of *like*. I'm yellow because I'm a motherfucking entrepreneur. I can't be bought by big city corporations. I'm my own man."

"And because God gave it to you," I added.

"Right on," he said.

"I always wanted to know what God looked like," Scarlet said. "I figure I'm going to get to see him soon enough, but I've always been one of those people who wants to know what I'm getting into before I sign on the dotted line."

"I'll be honest, dude," Raf said. "He wasn't what I expected. He's not the best looking guy in the world. I think the universe scrambled his face before it sent him to earth. And what's with the suits? I was expecting robes or a toga. And he can be a real dick if he's in a bad mood, especially if you accidentally lose something that's really expensive."

"I'll have to rethink that then," Scarlet said. "I lose expensive stuff all the time. If that's the tipping point between heaven and hell, then I guess I know where I'm headed."

I closed my eyes and muttered, "We're all headed there after this conversation."

"What did you lose?" Scarlet asked.

Raf shrugged. "I dunno. They never tell me.

Something important, I guess. But sometimes my memory isn't so great. I think it was a holiday, because I only smoke blunts on holidays. Otherwise it messes with my productivity. But turns out they wanted me to work on the holiday, and I was like, "No way, man. I want workers comp. So they gave me like, a thousand dollars extra, and then I went to work and lost their shit 'cause I was too high. I figure it's their own fault."

I was pretty sure that Raf thought Ugly Mo was God. I decided to play a hunch and see what happened.

"Hey, Raf, do you know Stella? She told me you gave awesome rides."

"Dude, why didn't you tell me Stella was your people? She's the best, man. Always gives Raf a baggie of the good stuff on top of my paycheck."

"What kind of good stuff?" Scarlet asked. "You got any Oracle?"

"Shit, woman. Oracle is an urban legend. Nobody can get their hands on oracle."

Scarlet dug around in her handbag and pulled out a baggie of marijuana. "It's as real as I'm standing here," she said. "You just gotta know how to get it. I'm rich, so I got lots of connections, on account of people like my money."

"Put that away," I hissed. "That's illegal."

"I got a prescription," Scarlet said.

"Not in this state," I said. "They'll arrest you."

"No one's going to arrest a ninety-year-old la-dy. I've got immunity. Besides, I need it for my arthritis. Otherwise my joints get all stiff and I can't move. I'm thinking about lighting up as soon as I get back to the hotel. I'm thinking my wizard's sleeve is in need of a healing spell, if you catch my drift."

I shook my head in disbelief. The best inter-preter on the planet wouldn't have had a clue what she was talking about.

"Why are you trying to stifle my constitutional rights, you old fuddy-duddy," she said, looking at me. "I fought for this country."

"Preach it, sister," Raf said.

"You're ninety years old," I told her. "You can do whatever you want. But there's a couple of cops on horseback roaming about that might not be so tolerant if you're waving it around in public."

"That's true, dude," Raf said. "They don't al-ways appreciate the magic. Sometimes they take you to the slammer and confiscate all your stuff.

Jail doesn't have good energy."

"Hmmph," Scarlet said and stuffed the bag back in her purse.

"I bet this is an entertaining job," I told him. "I bet you see and hear all kinds of things."

"Oh man. More than you know. But I'm kind of like a priest. Or Dr. Phil. I gotta keep the trust, man."

"Yeah, Stella told me things got pretty wild with that guy last Friday."

Raf went into a fit of giggles and he had to pull to the side of the road until he could get himself back under control.

"Dude…that was insane. Stella told me beforehand that things were going to get pretty hot and heavy and I just had to keep pedaling." Raf got distracted and started singing the "Just Keep Swimming" song from *Finding Nemo*, only he changed the word swimming to pedaling.

"Yeah, she said the guy was a real prick," I improvised.

"Stella can handle a dick," Raf said, breaking into giggles again. "No pun intended. It was a real difficult job too. I had to concentrate and keep out of the crowds. Dude was a moaner. Totally embarrassing."

"I bet," I said overselling it. "Still don't know how y'all got him out of here when he passed out. That must've been intense."

"Nah, it was no big." We were about a block from the Hamilton Inn. "This is like, total déjà vu. This is the same hotel I dropped them at."

"Whoa," I said, deadpan. If Raf wasn't the perfect example of the Say No To Drugs campaign, I didn't know what was.

"I know. But like I said, it was no big. Do you know Kimmie?" he asked.

"No, but I've heard so much about her," I lied.

"Meh, she's okay, I guess." Raf shrugged. "But she's on the housekeeping staff, so she let us in that side door there and up the stairs. No cameras in the stairwells, and Stella said we had to be super sneaky cause the dude was rich and married and his wife would be mad. See, we're like philanthropists."

"Hmm," I said. "What does Kimmie look like? Maybe we'll run into her while we're here."

"I dunno," he shrugged. "She's a girl. Like from Clueless."

"She's rich?" I asked.

"No, she's a real bitch. Lots of curly blonde hair. Mega tits. Like, *super* mega. Wouldn't mind motor-boating those puppies. And she's got one of those little moles at the corner of her mouth. Like that supermodel."

Raf stopped the pedi-cab right in front of the hotel and I gave him forty bucks.

"Rad," he said.

"Thanks for the ride," I said.

Raf and Scarlet were exchanging some kind of information that I probably didn't want to know about, so I headed inside the hotel. I'd seen the van parked in the back corner of the lot with Rosemarie sitting behind the wheel, waiting on us to arrive.

The lobby of the hotel was beige with splashes of burnt orange spread throughout the rugs and throw pillows and weird modern art on the walls. It was deserted and there was only one man behind the registration desk. I was guessing a Monday night in January wasn't all it was cracked up to be on the economy hotel circuit.

The man was tall and shaped like a pear, and his sandy hair was thin and stuck out about an inch all over so he looked like an overgrown Chia

Pet. His nametag said Kevin, and he was the manager.

"Are you checking in?" he asked with a smile.

He checked me out from head to toe and his smile turned smarmy. I resisted the urge to shudder.

"No, but I'm wondering if Kimmie's here? I've been driving around for a couple of weeks with a box of her stuff in the back of my car. I thought I'd just swing by and give it to her since I'm in the area."

His smile dimmed at the mention of Kimmie's name. "Kimmie is no longer employed here," he said stiffly. "We had an incident on the grounds a little over a week ago, and I guess it disturbed her. She quit a couple of days later. Didn't even give us two weeks, so we're shorthanded."

"Yeah, that pretty much sounds like her," I said sympathetically. "Try getting back rent from her."

I left with a wave and headed back to the parking lot. I stopped to text Kate and Savage and let them know what I'd found out from Raf about Stella and Kimmie. At least we were getting some names. And I also let them know that Ugly Mo had very possibly been playing me all along. I was guessing it wasn't an accident that Raf called him God.

In a sense, that was what it was all about. One omnipotent being that no one could touch, moving his pawns around the chessboard. Taking away life and giving life.

Kate answered the text with a thumbs up emoji, so I dropped my phone back into my handbag and went to get Scarlet.

I looked right and left, but the pedi-cab and Scarlet were nowhere in sight. I glanced over at Rosemarie, still sitting in the driver's seat of the van. She caught my eye and pointed to the side of the building, a scandalized look on her face. I sighed and walked toward the area where she'd pointed.

The smell was unmistakable, and so were the high-pitched giggles. The bright yellow pedi-cab was sitting under the only light on that side of the hotel and Raf and Scarlet were getting cozy in the back, passing a joint back and forth between them.

"Aunt Scarlet," I said.

She turned to look at me and then waved, her smile a little loopy. "Addison!" she said. "My vagina feels much better."

"I'm glad to hear it. But we really need to go. Maybe you could let Raf finish that off as a peace offering."

"Right-o," Scarlet said, giving Raf the joint. "Gotta go."

CHAPTER SEVENTEEN

Tuesday (sometime in the middle of the night)

B Y THE TIME I came out of my deep sleep, it was too late.

I wasn't sure what had woken me. It wasn't a sound. More the absence of sound. The rumble from the heat vents was missing. There was no buzz of electricity. Just dead silence. And the feeling that I wasn't alone.

I tried to keep my breathing steady and my panic at a minimum. But someone had broken into the agency, cut the electricity, and slipped into my office without waking me. And they'd done it quickly, because the second the electricity went out, an alert would've been sent to the alarm company.

My gun was at the edge of the mattress, but the second I moved they'd know I was awake and be ready. Then it didn't matter, because I felt the

sharp prick of a needle in my arm and then
nothing at all.

WHEN I WOKE again the pain in my skull was like
nothing I'd ever experienced and my vision was so
blurry it took me several minutes to realize I was
staring at a beige ceiling and not the gates of
heaven, which was good news, because I had much
higher expectations for heaven.

I rolled my eyes from side to side because it
was too painful to move my head, and recognition
started to kick in—shower curtain—toilet—
sink—dingy towels—*tray full of sharp surgical
instruments*. One of those things didn't belong.

My gaze froze on the tray, and I felt the panic
start to take over. My teeth chattered uncontrollably, and I couldn't seem to function—couldn't get
my wits about me. Not having my wits about me
wasn't unusual, but this time it was serious. I was
in deep trouble. And my charm and adorable
personality weren't going to get me out of this
mess.

I stared into the tub and my lungs constricted.
Blood pumped with a roaring whoosh in my ears,

and I tried desperately to suck in a breath. I was naked. And buried in an ice bath.

High-pitched wheezes escaped from my lips until I sounded similar to a balloon having the air slowly leaked from it. This was not good. In fact, this was about as far from good as I'd ever been. If my tear ducts hadn't been frozen I probably would've cried.

I rolled my head to the side and tried to listen—to see if I was alone or if my surgeons were still present. But nothing greeted me but silence and my erratic heartbeat.

The sign on the door was crudely written with black marker, and it said, *Call 9-1-1. Now.* An envelope with my name written on it was taped just beneath the sign.

Bile rose in my throat and little black dots were dancing like dust motes in front of my eyes. It was everything I could do to keep the contents of my stomach down. If I even had a stomach. I had no idea what kind of wounds the ice was covering, but I was almost one-hundred percent sure that vomiting wouldn't be good for it.

I looked at the surgical tray where there was supposed to be a phone, but there was nothing there—only sharp-edged instruments that mocked me. Panic clawed at me again. My ice was going to melt and I was going to bleed out, and I'd die alone in a bathtub in a three-and-a-half star hotel. I'd always imagined I'd die with a bit more glamour. It was kind of a letdown.

I couldn't die like this. My unwritten biography demanded I not end my story this way. My only choice was to try to move. To escape the tub and crawl my way out to the hallway where someone might find me before it was too late.

I was going to fall apart at some point, but not yet. I needed to survive. I had things in my life I still wanted to do. Like make out with Chris Hemsworth and get laser hair removal.

I focused on my body and tried to move my limbs, even if just a little. I managed to get my knee bent so it stuck up out of the ice bath, and it was then I noticed the plastic bag that surfaced with the movement. It took me a couple of tries to get my fingers to curl and pick up the bag, but once I did I was back to almost bursting into tears.

Inside the plastic bag was my cellphone, and there was only one person I could think of calling. Someone who would drop everything and come for me because I asked. Someone I didn't mind seeing me naked. Believe it or not, it was a short list.

My fingers fumbled at the opening of the plastic bag and I prayed like crazy that I didn't drop it in the water. Getting out of the tub at this point wasn't an option. I needed whatever insides I had left to stay put.

Wild animal sounds escaped my mouth as I dialed with shaking hands. It seemed to take forever as the phone rang—and rang—and rang. Then the sweetest voice I'd ever heard answered the phone.

But when I opened my mouth no words came out. Just hot air and desperation. I was well and truly fucked.

"Addison?" Nick said, the worry in his voice unmistakable.

All I could do was breathe into the phone. My teeth were chattering so hard I couldn't speak.

"Addison, is that you?" he asked again. "Who is this?"

I made a sound that came out something like a newborn goat, and then a sob escaped in my frustration.

"Addison, honey, if that's you, I want you to take some deep breaths. You're fine and I'm going to come get you, okay? I just need you to tell me where you are. I'm coming to get you."

Nick's soothing words helped get my panic under control. I was alive. That was the important thing. If I wanted to stay alive then I needed to help him so he could help me.

My eyes moved wildly toward the little sink where the shampoo and soaps were sitting. I had a feeling I was back at the Hamilton Inn, but I needed to confirm it.

"N-Nick," I said, teeth chattering. "P-pl-please."

"Okay, baby," he said, his sigh of relief so audible I could hear it through the phone. "We're all here. I'm going to come and get you. Do you know where you are?"

The letter Y was really difficult to say for some reason, so I couldn't get the word *yes* past my lips. I grunted instead.

"Okay, good," he continued. "Kate is right here next to me. We're all here looking for you. She wants me to ask if you're at the Hamilton Inn. Just grunt again if it's a yes. Stay silent if no."

I grunted again, and I heard a lot of movement on the other end. Nick was on his way. He was coming and we'd get through this together. Together was all that mattered.

It felt like the wait was endless, but Nick stayed on the line with me, talking nonsense the entire time to fill the silence. My teeth chattered audibly now and speaking was impossible. The cold was exhausting and my head kept lolling to the side.

And then I heard it. The sound of voices outside and the key card being slipped into the door. Then it opened and Nick was there in the bathroom with me. He scanned the scene quickly, not missing anything, and then he was kneeling beside me.

I was crying now, big silent tears that I couldn't have held back if I'd wanted to.

"It's going to be fine," Nick said, but I noticed his hands were shaking as he leaned in to kiss my forehead. "I'm going to drain the water and then we can see what we're dealing with."

I just stared at him. I was tired all over and nodding would've taken too much effort. My teeth chattered again violently and I watched as he stuck his hand in the tub, the icy water coming past his elbow, and heard the glug of the drain as he pulled the stopper.

I saw the EMTs hovering behind Nick, ready to take action, but I was so tired my vision blurred.

"Addison," Nick said. I had the feeling he'd been calling my name for a while. He patted me on the cheek lightly and another shiver wracked my body. "The water's all gone. You've been drugged, which is why you're having so much trouble staying awake. But they didn't take anything. It's only been a couple of hours since the alarm alerted us, so they didn't have time to do the surgery. It was just a warning."

"W-worked," I said, shaking violently again.

"The paramedics are going to get you out and take you to the hospital to be checked. Did you happened to see any faces?" he asked.

I shook my head no, because it was all I could do, and then the paramedics were moving Nick out of the way so they could do their job. I hardly cared at all that I was naked.

CHAPTER EIGHTEEN

Wednesday (early afternoon)

I WAS MAD. I was still cold too. And cold and mad didn't go together one bit.

I was sitting at the conference table at the agency, surrounded by Nick, Savage, Kate, Jimmy Royal, Lucy, and Rosemarie. I wasn't sure why Rosemarie was there, but she hadn't left my side since I'd been admitted to the hospital the day before.

I'd finally convinced my mother and Aunt Scarlet to go home and get some rest. Scarlet felt awful that she'd been bamboozled by Ugly Mo, and my mother was trying to deal with the shock that she had a daughter in the hospital *and* that she was having to come face-to-face with Aunt Scarlet. It was a trial for all parties involved.

"Explain to me again why Ugly Mo isn't the target," I said, furious.

"Because you've got to get all the little fish to lure the big fish," Savage said. "He all but admitted to you that he was involved. He even gave you the woman in Atlanta to send you running after that trail. Look at the network that he's got set up. Think about all the contradictions.

"It wasn't coincidence that Mo called Jimmy and told him about a new van being ready, and that he'd sell it at a great price if anyone new at the agency needed a surveillance vehicle. It wasn't coincidence that he kept in contact with Scarlet, so he could keep up with you. It wasn't coincidence that he's so well-known at the Olde Pink House. You said yourself you were amazed at how he blended in, depending on where he was. The restaurant was a set-up from the beginning. I guarantee, everyone from the clients who met them there to this Stella woman are all involved in the black market transplant operation. Ugly Mo owns the city," Savage said. "At least most of it. And he owns the people in it."

"Okay, so we can't touch Ugly Mo. There's no proof, because he hasn't gotten his hands dirty," I said. "How do we round up all the other players if there are so many?"

"That's the question," Kate said, "I'm not altogether sure that Anthony Dunnegan didn't know more than he's saying going in. He said he was meeting with clients about a merger they backed out on. We need to find out what clients and what the merger was."

"Boggy ground," Nick said, wincing.

"Which is why we'll take care of it instead of the cops," Kate said with a sharp smile. "I'm not so concerned about laws just now."

"We need to find Stella," I said. "She's the key. She's the one who's putting herself on the line by being identifiable. If we can get to her, there's no reason why she wouldn't roll on others."

"Ugly Mo is smart," Savage said. "We've been watching him a long time. He's gone all this time with nothing but suspicion surrounding his name. You can bet none of those people could point to him and say Mo specifically gave them orders. Mo doesn't mind sacrificing his own. They can't go anywhere else anyway. He brands them so they're unusable to any other potential employee."

"No wonder he knew so much about how Fat Louie did business," I said, getting angrier by the second. I hated being duped. And I especially hated it, because for a short moment of time, I'd gone to bat for the guy.

"I agree that we need to find Stella," Kate said. "If she can give us some names, we can at least hold them long enough to make Mo think they spilled everything. They won't want to leave jail. Because when Mo picks them up he'll put them through an interrogation we could never hope to compete with."

"I can help with that," Savage said. "I spent my time yesterday trying to run all the leads on her."

Savage clicked the remote and the screen came down from the ceiling and a woman's image was projected on it. My mouth dropped open in surprise.

"It's Wonder Woman," I said. She really did look uncannily like her.

"Also known as Stella Pedrotti. She's the coordinator for the national transplant list. Every name and case is given to her, and she decides who goes higher on the list based on need."

"Perfect," I said. "Where is she?"

"She lives here in Savannah. And is happily married to Richard Drake."

"Richard Drake?" I said, wondering why the

name sounded so familiar. "Ohmigosh. The manager at Olde Pink House. No wonder they were so familiar with each other." And then I thought about it. "Richard Drake let his wife sleep with that slimeball Dunnegan?"

"They do what Mo tells them to do," Savage said.

"Then what are we waiting for?" I asked. "Let's go get them."

"Richard and Stella are currently out of town, according to their credit card statements and airline tickets. In fact, they left town just after Richard finished speaking with you the other day. A couple of days in New York for a fundraiser to raise awareness for becoming an organ donor."

"Well, that's convenient."

"Not really," Savage said. "But we've got the alert out."

CHAPTER NINETEEN

I HADN'T REALLY been in the mood for company after the meeting had adjourned. Everyone had a job to do and tasks to run down. But not me. I was supposed to rest. I *hated* resting. And I hated that everyone else was keeping busy, while I was left twiddling my thumbs. Mostly I was feeling sorry for myself.

So I got in my van and started driving. I probably drove for two hours, mulling over everything that had happened. Then I found a nice spot along the Savannah River and I parked and watched the water flow. And then I made a list. I loved lists. Adored them. And my mind always cleared when I saw an itemized list of things.

I wrote down everything that had happened to me since I took the Anthony Dunnegan case—a precise timeline of events and the names of everyone involved.

There was something I wanted to check, so I called the number Eloise Hunt had given me for while they were staying in France. It was late evening there and I hoped she was still awake.

She answered in French, and I heaved a sigh of relief.

"Mrs. Hunt, I'm sorry to bother you, but this is Addison Holmes. The private investigator from Savannah."

"Sure, Ms. Holmes. Have you found my husband's killer?"

"Not yet, but I believe we're getting closer. Would you mind telling me if you and your husband took out new life insurance policies recently?"

"Why, yes. I guess a little over a year ago. It was a legitimate policy. They honored it and the check was divided into the children's trust funds. I didn't need the money, since our assets just shifted to me, and vice-versa if I'd gone first, so we made the children our beneficiaries."

"Did someone come out to the house to give you a medical exam and take blood for the policies?"

"Sure, I think they have to when the policy is

over a million dollars."

"I don't suppose you have that paperwork with the name of the nurse who came to your home?"

"Not here in Paris," she said. "But my estate manager is still in the States. I can call him and he can email you anything you need."

"That would be great, thanks." I disconnected and was feeling a little more energetic, so I drove through a Dairy Queen and got a steak finger basket. I also got a hot fudge sundae and ate it first, so it didn't melt while I was eating my lunch. It turned out that was a mistake, because I spent a few minutes with my muscles going into spasms when the cold hit it again. The good thing about driving the van was when that happened I could go take a nap in the bed.

By the time I woke it was dusk and my phone was full of missed calls and text messages. I immediately let everyone know I was all right and then checked my email. Eloise Hunt's estate manager had, indeed, sent an email. The name of the nurse who'd done the bloodwork on the Hunts was the same nurse who did the bloodwork for the Dun-

negans. That was a coincidence that most definitely couldn't be overlooked. Her name was Kimberly
Eastman.

I opened my laptop and logged into the agency
database. And then I did a background search on
Kimberly Eastman. When her photograph popped
up I would've fist bumped anyone who'd been
sitting in the general vicinity, I was so excited.
Kimberly had a lot of curly blonde hair, mega tits,
and a mole at the corner of her mouth. Just like
Kimmie from the Hamilton Inn.

I pulled her recent credit card transactions and
looked to see if she was still in town. Or at least
close by. She'd made a purchase less than an hour
ago of more than two-hundred dollars' worth of
groceries at the Piggly Wiggly. A woman didn't
buy that many groceries if she was planning on
leaving town.

A plan was forming in my mind that I knew
was a horrible idea, but I couldn't seem to help
myself. So I called Rosemarie and Scarlet and
asked if they were in. Then I asked them again just
to make sure. What I planned didn't leave room
for quitters.

I had an address and a photograph, and I was

still pissed from what had happened to me the day before. I was ready for revenge.

NORMALLY, I'D ASK Kate to join in on something like I had planned, but Kate really cared about the agency and I figured the more she could distance herself from me if I got caught the better. That left Scarlet and Rosemarie.

I invited Scarlet because I figured she had experience with this sort of thing. I still wasn't sure why I'd invited Rosemarie along, but she'd be good moral support in any case, and she could keep a secret if it was important.

Scarlet had invited Rosemarie to take the second bedroom in her suite since we'd be getting back so late, so I picked them both up a little after seven o'clock at the Ballastone. There were some pretty amazing things about working for a detective agency. What I learned my first day on the job was that no one really had any privacy. If you knew where and how to look, your entire life was right there for everyone to see. And there was no such thing as a secure email account.

So what I knew about Kimberly Easton was

that she'd bought a big bill of groceries with the plan to stay in for dinner. And from another credit card purchase, she planned to meet someone for a nine o'clock movie at the Regal Cinema. She'd purchased two tickets.

I pulled in front of the hotel to pick up Scarlet and Rosemarie, and I almost screamed when they popped out of the bushes next to the historic hotel. They were both dressed from head to toe in black. Scarlet was wearing a balaclava over her head and Rosemarie had on a black baseball cap that spelled BITCH in rhinestones across the front.

They both got in the back of the van and I drove away before they'd gotten the door closed completely. I was in all black too. There was no room for color in an old school smackdown.

"I had to borrow the hat from my neighbor," Rosemarie said. "I don't wear a lot of black, and there wasn't time to go shopping."

"It's fine," Scarlet said, her thin lips showing through the mouth hole of the balaclava. "It adds a little variety to the program. It's best to keep them off-guard. You don't ever want them to know where the next punch is going to land."

"We're not going to make her bleed, are we?"

Rosemarie asked. "Because you remember I don't do so well with blood."

I remembered. The last time we came across a body Rosemarie threw up on the crime scene and passed out. The cops hadn't been happy.

Scarlet punched her fist into her open palm, looking fierce. "We do whatever it takes. We're bringing these sons of bitches down. To think I let my Venus fly trap get pounded for nothing. He was just using me. And nobody uses Scarlet Holmes like that."

They were both getting worked up, and I could admit that I was a little excitable too. I couldn't stop fidgeting, and I was sweating like a nun in a brothel under all the black layers. I also wasn't so sure I had the torture gene in me. In theory, I was excellent at shaking someone down. In reality, I didn't have a clue where to start or what to do. Not unless I was giving her a thousand paper cuts. I could probably do that one, but I have a pretty short attention span, so I might only make it to ten or fifteen.

Kimberly Easton had a home in Georgetown. She lived in a neighborhood with fairly large houses on large wooded lots. And she lived at the end of the street. I killed the headlights as we drove down her street and we found a place to park so the van was half hidden by bushes. It was getting her into the van that was going to take coordination.

The lights were on in Kimberly's house, and at precisely eight o'clock she shut off all but the foyer lights and came out the front door, locking it behind her.

"Step on it!" Scarlet yelled. "You're going to miss your window of opportunity."

I slammed my foot on the gas and we shot forward. I heard a crash in the back and realized they'd both been standing in preparation of the kidnapping.

I squealed to a halt next to Kimberly's BMW and Rosemarie and Scarlet leaned out the side door, making a grab for her. Kimberly let out a shriek and Scarlet tossed a bag over her head while Rosemarie muscled her into the van.

"Yippee ki-yay, motherfuckers!" Scarlet yelled, slamming the side door shut.

I pressed the gas pedal all the way to the floor and took off, knocking all three of the back passengers on their asses. I had to slow down. This would be awfully hard to explain to the police if I got pulled over, even if I was Nick's possible fiancée.

We drove all the way down to Whiskey Bayou and parked the van in a secluded marsh area we'd played in as kids. As long as we didn't get out of the van, we probably wouldn't get eaten by alligators or snakes.

They'd Duck Taped Kimmie to one of the captains' chairs while I'd been driving, and I giggled with hysteria when I finally parked the van and saw our captive. I'd told Rosemarie and Scarlet to bring what they had on hand for a kidnapping and inquisition. The woman had a sleep mask over her eyes and a ball gag in her mouth from the little gifts they'd given us at the theater when we went to see Fifty Shades of Grey. The fuzzy handcuffs were clamped around her wrists.

"I might be having a panic attack," Rosemarie said. "And I have to go to the bathroom."

"There's toilet paper in there now," I told her. "I borrowed some from the agency."

Rosemarie scurried back to the bathroom and I had a feeling she was going to be in there a while. That left me and Scarlet to get the job done.

Scarlet took off the eye mask and the ball gag so Kimberly could answer our questions.

"You people are insane," she hissed.

"We're insane?" I said incredulously. "I woke up in a fucking bathtub full of ice yesterday. Why don't you tell me how insane I am again?"

The woman blanched and I was thinking I might actually be good at intimidation tactics. "I don't know what you're talking about," she said.

"Sure you do," I said. "You know, this whole black market transplant thing. We'd like you to just answer truthfully if you don't mind. This is a new van and I'm not too keen on getting fluids on the upholstery."

The woman stared stonily at me and I wondered what I was supposed to do next. Fortunately, Scarlet took things in hand. She pulled a large, brown paper bag from beneath one of the seats and started unpacking it on the table.

"That's fine," Scarlet said, her voice friendly. "You don't want to talk you don't have to talk. We'll just do a few things to you until you feel the need to spill your guts about Ugly Mo, Stella, and Richard, and how you fit into this whole mess."

"Fuck you," Kimberly said.

"That's just damned rude," Scarlet said. "Watch your fucking mouth."

Then she started pullin the things out of the sack, one by one, and my eyes widened. An apple corer, a sheet of sand paper, a hand mixer, paint thinner, and clothes pins. I couldn't decide if we were about to torture someone or start a DIY project.

Kimmie was starting to look a little worried. I was feeling a little worried too.

"That's a real nice manicure you got there," Scarlet said, taking one of her cuffed hands. "Must be a real challenge to get those little dolphins painted on there."

"They're all hand-painted," Kimmie said suspiciously.

Scarlet's grip tightened on her hand and then she grabbed the sandpaper, rubbing it across the top of her nails as fast as she could.

"What are you doing?" Kimmie yelled, trying to squirm out of Scarlet's grasp. "What kind of monster are you?"

The smell of the sandpaper and friction was strong, and little particles of fingernail dust were flying through the air.

"My niece is going to ask you some questions," Scarlet said. "I suggest you answer them or you won't have anything but bloody nubs by the time I'm through with you. I bet you've got a pedicure too, huh?"

Kimmie let out a muffled sob and looked at me, imploring me to save her.

"Umm," I said. "It's too late for you, Kimmie. We've started putting it together and all of you peons are going to get taken down. You know Ugly Mo doesn't care. I bet he's got your replacements waiting in the wings."

Kimmie face paled at the mention of Mo. "I don't know who Mo is."

"You must really be scared of him to not care if you go to prison. I guess he must be worth protecting. Of course, it would probably be pretty scary for you if word got back to Mo that you tried to rat him out. I bet accidents happen all the time in prison."

I saw Scarlet beaming at me. I could tell it was a proud moment for her. I wasn't feeling so proud of myself, however. The thought of getting revenge wasn't nearly as exciting as it had been earlier in the day.

"No, you can't do that," she said, the fear real in her eyes.

"Here's what we know," I said. "We know Stella has control of that donor list. She sees every name, their financial status, and how rare their needs are. Then there's you, scoping out potential donors through million-dollar life insurance policies. I guess it must be pretty exciting to get the results of the rare blood work come in and know that the person has been marked for death. Pretty exhilarating isn't it."

Kimmie stayed silent and hatred was beginning to replace the look of fear in her eyes.

"How did you and Stella meet?" I asked her.

Kimmie rolled her eyes. "We went to college together. We've been friends forever. You're wrong about Ugly Mo," she said. "Nobody can just step in and do what we do. You'll never prove any of our involvement. We'll stand together like always. There's too much money at stake."

Scarlet put down the sandpaper and picked up the paint thinner. Then she ran her fingers through Kimmie's blonde curly hair. She unscrewed the lid the the paint thinner and the smell was powerful enough to bring tears to my eyes.

"Those are hair extensions aren't they?" Scarlet asked. "Paint thinner is great for breaking down the polymer. Of course, it's still going to hurt like heck when I yank them out of your head."

"You're a devil woman," Kimmie said, pushing away from Scarlet the closer she came. "Don't put that in my hair. You'll destroy me. I've got a date this weekend."

"You're only date is going to be a bitch named Wanda in the clinker," Scarlet said, her eyes beady and mean.

"I'll talk! I'll talk!" Kimmie said, her sobs uncontrollable.

This was not how my interpretation of the interrogation process had gone in my mind. I'd been expecting something a little more…violent.

"Who's the surgeon?" I asked. "Another college friend?"

"Yes," Kimmie said, slumping forward in her chair, her hair hanging down over her face. "Ashley Dunnegan."

"What?" I asked, the shock on my face unmistakable. "Anthony Dunnegan's wife?"

"Yes," Kimmie answered.

"That can't be," I said. "I read over Ashley

Dunnegan's file when I looked through Anthony's background. She's a socialite. She's never worked a day in her life."

"Because that dickwad Anthony wouldn't let her," Kimmie said, rolling her eyes. "We all met during freshman year rush at University of Georgia. Ashley was pre-med and the smartest of all of us. She met Anthony her senior year and he charmed her until she was blind in love. The rest of us could see what a snake he was, but not Ashley.

"She started medical school after graduation and Anthony started law school. He was already cheating on her, but she never believed it. He hated the hours she had to put in, especially when she got into her fourth year. She was gone all the time and never had time to spend with him. So he'd console himself with a bunch of floozies on the side.

Ashley had decided she wanted to be a heart surgeon, and she was good at it. She would've graduated at the top of her class. And then during the last semester Anthony proposed to her and told her how important his career was going to be and all about his political ambitions. I'm sure you've heard he has his eye on the senate."

"It's been mentioned," I said, thinking of Nick's grandfather.

"Stella and I tried to talk her out of it, but she said part of marriage was making sacrifices, and if Anthony thought they'd be better off with her being a full time hostess and wife to move his career forward, then that's what she'd do. So she dropped out."

"How long was it before she found out he was cheating on her?" I asked.

"Just a couple of years. She was devastated. He'd stopped trying to even hide it, and the women he slept with didn't try to keep things quiet either. She'd thrown away her whole life for a man who didn't give a shit. And that's when we started putting our heads together. Anthony is a dick, but he's an amazing attorney. She'd signed a pre-nup when they'd married because he'd told her he was set to inherit a lot of money from his grandparents, which was bullshit, but she signed it anyway. So we knew if she was going to leave him then she had to have a nest egg of her own that he couldn't find or touch.

"I was already working as a nurse and Stella

had her MBA and was hired by the American Transplant Foundation. Stella is smart as hell, so it wasn't long before she was basically running the whole thing. And one night after a few glasses of wine and another bitch session about Anthony, the idea came to us. And it worked.

"Then all of a sudden we were coordinating more business than we knew what to do with and trying to figure out how to deal with all the money. We were only dealing with kidneys in the early days, and as brilliant as Ashley was, it had been a couple years since she'd been in the medical field so she had to practice on a couple of patients before she really started to get the hang of it.

"Then one day we each get an email telling us that we were being bought out. That we would continue our work as is, and in exchange this company would take care of the money side of things and hide it from the IRS and our spouses if we wished. This company would be a silent partner of sorts, and take care of all the hard stuff for us, and in exchange they'd take half the profit.

"We kind of freaked out at that because we weren't charging as much in the early days as we are now. But the email told us we'd be making our services more exclusive. To higher risk patients who needed our services more. And that they'd pay more to stay alive."

"It didn't bother you that you'd be taking one life to save another?" I asked.

"Of course it did," she said. "At first. But the email had some attachments. We all had small children at that point and there were pictures of our kids at the park and at school." Big tears ran down her cheeks. "We really didn't have any choice. Our children weren't worth the risk. And then it just became a job like any other. We had a system down, and we did what we had to do. And we made a lot of money on top of it. Now our kids are grown and none of them will ever have to want for anything."

She looked like she was trying to convince herself more than she was trying to convince me.

"And I guess Ashley didn't mind doing the surgery on her own husband," I said. "Handy how that worked out."

Kimmie genuinely smiled at that. "That was just plain good luck. It was less than a year ago that Anthony up and decided that they needed to get a life insurance policy since they were getting older. They'd never had one before because there'd never been a need with the amount of income he makes. Ashley would've been set for life if anything had happened to Anthony.

"But he wanted to get a policy. She figured he'd finally found a woman that she was worth leaving for, but with him having such high political aspirations he wouldn't have wanted a divorce, so she'd need to die for the new Mrs. Dunnegan to be put in place.

"I had a colleague go out to the house instead of me to do the medicals, but when I showed Ashley the result of his blood type you would've thought she'd won the lottery. She thought it would be a much better punishment to leave him alive than to kill him, so she took his kidney."

The toilet flushed and we all looked up startled. I'd completely forgotten that Rosemarie had gone to the bathroom. The water ran and then she came out, a wet paper towel pressed to her forehead.

"Sorry about that," she said. "I think I'm ready now. I just had to psych myself up for this. I'm not a natural torturer like Scarlet."

And the Rosemarie screwed her eyes shut and

balled her hand into a fist, popping Kimmie right in the jaw and knocking her out cold.

Rosemarie shook her hand and yelled in pain as the bones crunched, but then she looked at me. "How was that?"

"Nice shot. It's a good thing we got all the information out of her before you knocked her out."

"I AM UTTERLY speechless," Kate said, staring down at restrained Kimmie.

I'd called Kate to ask for advice while Kimmie had still been unconscious. She hadn't been happy when she'd woken, her jaw swollen and bruised.

"I sure wish she was," Rosemarie said, pointing to Kimberly. "She's done nothing but whine since she woke up." Rosemarie's upper lip was dotted with sweat and her hair was soaking wet under her BITCH cap.

It was getting a little crowded in the van, but the four of us hauling a woman strapped to a chair would probably draw more attention that we wanted.

"Look, just get me out of this van," Kimmie begged. "I'll sign a statement. I'll flip on everyone involved. But get me away from these crazy bitches. I'm begging you."

Kate stared at her a few seconds and then looked at us. "I guess that's a deal we can work with. It won't bring down Ugly Mo, but it'll shut down the other operations and everyone involved will go to jail."

My phone rang and I saw Savage's name pop up on the caller ID. "Do I want to know what's going on down there?" he asked.

"It's probably best you don't," I said. "But Kimberly Easton has confessed and agreed to testify against the others."

"That's very efficient of you," he said, and then there was a short amount of silence before he said, "You know you can always come to me for help, no matter what answer you give Nick, right?"

I breathed out a sigh of relief. I'd actually become pretty attached to Savage over the last months. We worked well together.

"Yeah, I know."

He hung up and we helped Kate transport Kimberly to her car, and then we followed her back to Savannah at a law-abiding pace.

CHAPTER TWENTY

Thursday

I WAS EATING dinner with my mom and Vince and filling them in on the past few days of my life when Nick's call came in.

"It's Nick," I told them.

"Take it," my mom said. "You've put him through hell this week."

"Hey," I told him, nervous all of a sudden. Maybe I shouldn't have taken the call in front of an audience.

"Did you hear about Ugly Mo?" Nick asked.

"No, what happened?"

"We just responded to a call. Someone catapulted a firebomb right through his bedroom window. Apparently he always takes a nap this time of day and he was fast asleep on the bed. He and the bed went up like a tinderbox."

I froze and felt the blood drain from my face.

A catapult. Aunt Scarlet.

"Yeah, I'd never seen anything quite like it," Nick said. "It looked homemade. Used rosary beads to anchor it. Anyway, I'm going to be tied up working this for the foreseeable future. I'll give you a call tomorrow when I'm free."

"Sounds good," I said, still in shock. "Be safe." And then we disconnected.

I called the Ballastone and asked for Aunt Scarlet's room. I was told by the front desk that she'd already checked out and one of the cars had taken her to the airport.

I wasn't sure how I felt about that. But I was pretty sure I was the only one who knew that she was a killer.

EPILOGUE

Friday (My Birthday)

A MONTH AGO today Nick had gotten down on one knee and proposed marriage. It had been a beautiful moment, but interrupted. I wondered if things would've happened differently if we hadn't had that interruption. Would we be planning a wedding? Or would we have already been well on our way to mending our respective broken hearts.

I hadn't slept at all the night before, knowing that the day had finally come. And now that it had, I felt a resolve and finality in my decision that I hadn't felt in the days leading up to it.

I'd put the ring he'd given me locked in my desk drawer for safe keeping. I took it out now and flipped open the little black box that had DeLuce's written in silver script across the top. Almost a year before we'd sat in a jewelry shop, pretending to get engaged for a case, and the ring laying in my hand was the one that had made me wish for one fleeting second that it was real. But we hadn't been anywhere close to ready for marriage at that point. Several months later he gave me the ring for real.

The band was thick silver, and in the center sat a cluster of freshwater pearls the size of caviar surrounded by a circle of black diamonds. It was unique in every way, and it was perfect.

I flipped the lid closed and put the box in my handbag. Then I dressed in jeans and an oversized oxford shirt in blue, slipped on my Toms, and headed to the van, the weight of the ring in my purse tremendous.

It was a short drive to the Savannah-Chatham Police Department, and I found a spot in visitor parking. With my heart in my throat, I headed inside and waved to Angie Driskoll, who was manning the front desk.

I signed in and she waved me back. I'd been a common fixture at the police department for most of my life—visiting my dad on occasion and now Nick. It hadn't change in thirty-one years. It still smelled of burnt coffee and industrial strength cleaner, and the walls were still an ugly green that made everyone's skin tone look horrible.

The desks were clumped together in different divisions, and I walked down the long haul until I got to the door that said detectives. Then I took a deep breath and hoped to God I knew what the hell I was doing.

The detectives division was mostly deserted except for a Johnson and Lipinski, who were huddled together over something. I already knew it'd been a long night for Nick. He'd sent a text the day before letting me know he'd caught a bad one and he wasn't sure when he'd be free. I had enough friends at PD that it hadn't been hard to find out when he'd come back from the crime scene about an hour before.

He still wore yesterday's clothes and had way past a five o'clock shadow. His eyes were shadowed and hooded—cop eyes—and they gave nothing away as he talked rapidly with the phone pressed to his ear and then made a few notes. That same gaze hit me as I walked toward his desk, and I realized it must suck to see him coming during an interrogation.

I waited patiently for him to get off the phone, and I studied him as he finished up, noting the grief and exhaustion on his face.

He hung up and we stared at each other a few seconds, the gravity of the moment taking me a little by surprise.

"Addison," he said, standing so we were on equal ground. "I thought we'd meet up later. I've still got a couple of hours of paperwork to do before I can go home."

It was the first time since I'd met Nick that I could remember seeing nervousness in his face. He was scared to death of what would happen in the next moments, and dragging it out would only be a cruelty.

"I know you do," I said. "I heard about the case. I'm sorry."

"It's the job," he said, shrugging.

I cleared my throat and hoped I had the right words. "I came here for a reason. Cop life is in my blood," I said. "And we met because of who you are. Our paths never would've crossed otherwise. So I thought it appropriate that I come to you here."

I opened my handbag and pulled out the little black box. Nick didn't glance down at it. He just kept staring at me. I flipped it open and said, "It's a beautiful ring."

"Addison," he said.

The I handed the box out to him and he finally looked down at it. My hand was trembling. And then he gingerly took it from me, as if it were a bomb.

"You thought it appropriate that you do this here?" he asked, his voice strangely hoarse.

"Of course," I said. "You proposed to me once on bended knee, and I told me you wouldn't have to ask me again. That I'd just give you an answer. But I have to confess I enjoyed the moment, before we got interrupted, I mean. So if you wouldn't mind, I'd like you to ask me again."

I bit my lip and waited for him to say something. But he didn't. There was just silence. Johnson and Lipinski were staring at us raptly now, their attention no longer on the case they were working.

"You don't have to get down on your knee again," I clarified, rushing to fill the silence. "Unless you've maybe changed your mind about the whole thing, and if that's the case, I'm going to feel pretty stupid."

"Let me get this straight," he said, looking

back at me. "You're not returning the ring to me to keep?"

"Ohmigosh, no," I said, moving around to the other side of his desk. "I was giving it back to you so you could give it to me for real this time. And so I could accept it."

I didn't do well in situations like this. The way events played out in my mind were never quite the same as how they played out in real life. In my head, this had been a simple matter. In reality, I'd complicated things and scared the shit out of Nick in the meantime.

"Okay, I'm calling a do-over," I said abruptly. "But first I'm going to hug you, even though other cops are watching. I won't let it happen again." And then I threw my arms around him and held him close. I'd missed touching him. Not having that physical connection over the last month had been like torture. I didn't want to go through that again. And I didn't want to put Nick through that again.

But I couldn't regret the time. I knew for sure that I wanted to spend the rest of my life with the man in my arms.

"I can not believe you thought that was a good

idea to hand the ring to me that way," he said, squeezing me tight. "You've got no sense. But I love you to distraction."

"I like how you temper the insult with words of love."

"It's better than strangling you."

"Can I have my ring now? I've been staring at that thing in the box for a month."

"Since you've botched things so badly, it's my turn," he said, taking the ring out of the box. "Addison Holmes, I'm going to keep this short and sweet. I love you. And you love me. And we're going to get married."

I nodded at his no-nonsense approach. I was ready to officially be engaged and start planning a wedding. I was ready to start my life with this man.

"Yes," I said, grinning from ear to ear. "We're going to get married."

Nick took my hand in his and placed the ring on my finger. It looked like it belonged there, and I felt tears well in my eyes as emotion overcame me.

And then he dropped the bomb. "When I said we're getting married, I meant we're getting married a week from today. I'm not waiting for you any longer. You've got seven days to meet me in front of the preacher, or we can leave now and just elope. Your choice."

My smile vanished and my mouth fell open. The only thing I could think to say was, "My mother is going to kill you."

He leaned close until our lips almost touched and whispered, "I just don't give a damn."

Printed in Great Britain
by Amazon